RANDOM HOUSE
LARGE
PRINT

Second Act

Danielle Steel

Second Act

A Novel

RANDOM HOUSE
LARGE PRINT

Published in the United States of America by Random House Large Print in association with Delacorte Press, an imprint of Random House, a division of Penguin Random House LLC, New York.

Cover design: Lisa Amoroso
Cover images: © Knk Phl Prasan Kha Phibuly/EyeEm/ Getty Images (sky), © Justin Kase zsixz/ Alamy Stock Photo (couple), © Marcin Rogozinski/ Alamy Stock Photo (cottage and landscape)
Author photograph: © Michael Coste

The Library of Congress has established a Cataloging-in-Publication record for this title.

ISBN: 978-0-593-58788-1

www.penguinrandomhouse.com/large-print-format-books

FIRST LARGE PRINT EDITION

Printed in the United States of America

1st Printing

To my darling children,
Trevor, Todd, Beatrix, Nick,
Samantha, Victoria, Vanessa,
Maxx, and Zara,

May you find what matters most to you,
what you care about and love,
believe in and are willing to fight for.

May you be brave and strong enough
to follow the path you love,
with someone you love,
and who loves you.

I love you with all my heart,
                    Mom/d.s.

There will come a time
when you think everything is finished.
That will be the beginning.
—Louis L'Amour

Second Act

Chapter 1

The building that housed Global Studios in Century City was impressive, but going in through the private entrance to the office of the head of the studio, the CEO of Global, was like entering another universe. Or boarding a rocket ship to the moon. A security guard stood at the discreetly set-apart elevator to escort VIPs and use his badge on the inside security panel to give them access to Andy Westfield's office on the forty-fourth floor. No one could reach the CEO's private quarters on the top floor without an invitation. Visitors were checked carefully at the main desk, their IDs examined, their fingerprints and photographs taken, their names verified with the reception desk upstairs. By the time they reached the elevator, they had been thoroughly vetted. No attack had ever been attempted on the CEO at Global, but it had happened to other heads of studios, and security measures were particularly acute and high-tech surrounding Andy.

The private elevator shot up at high speed without a stop. Visitors then found themselves at another reception desk, where they were expected and warmly greeted. The reception area was beautifully decorated with leather couches and priceless contemporary art, and visitors rarely had long to wait. The doors opened automatically into a small anteroom with paintings from Andy's personal collection, and fourteen-foot red lacquered doors led into the inner sanctum where Andy sat in peaceful splendor at an enormous mahogany and steel desk with a view of all of Los Angeles. A long wall to his right spoke of his own history. There was a row of posters of his parents' famous movies. He was the only son of two of Hollywood's beloved legends. His father, the most famous cowboy who had ever lived in films, John Westfield, originally from Montana, had come to Hollywood at eighteen to be an actor, and was a cowboy to his very core. After thirty years as an actor, he fell in love with directing and became one of the great directors of iconic Westerns. He had won four Oscars as an actor and collected three more as a director. He was a man of strong principles and values, which came across to the audience on film. He had set a powerful example for Andy, and been an admirable husband and father. Tall, rugged, and handsome, he was the hero men respected, little boys wanted to be when they grew up, and women dreamed about. His wife, Andy's mother, Eva Lundquist, originally from Sweden, was one of the most glamorous stars in Hollywood in her day. She and John were an unlikely, spectacular, and successful pair. She had two Oscars to her credit as well, and retired young to marry John and have Andy. They had been the most loved couple in Hollywood history, and were a strong role model to their son.

Andy had his father's height and good looks, with blond hair and a chiseled face, which had weathered and aged well in his father's case, and a notable cleft chin. John was an enormous man with a cowboy's frame. His hair was darker than Andy's, who had his Swedish mother's fair Nordic coloring and bright blue eyes. Andy was blessed with his heredity. He was almost as tall as his father, and just as handsome. He had never longed to be an actor. He knew the toll it had taken on his parents, although they did their best to shield their family life from the paparazzi. But they were always there, lingering in the background.

Andy's talent as a screenwriter had become apparent early. He had gone to USC and studied film. He had an undeniable gift. He spent the summers in college working on the sets of his father's movies, and after he graduated from USC he had written two scripts for his father. He'd had a sixteen-year career behind the scenes as a screenwriter, when he got sidetracked into the Hollywood power game. Because of his parents, doors opened to him that wouldn't have otherwise, and the opportunities rapidly became too tempting to turn down. His father had warned him to be careful but seize the opportunities he was given as they came and choose those that would best serve him. Andy had chosen wisely, often with his father's advice.

When AMCO, a major industrial corporation, bought Global Studios to glamorize their image, they sought out Andy and he became the youngest studio head in the business at thirty-eight. It was a heady experience and he handled it well. He put screenwriting behind him and dedicated himself to the business. At fifty-seven, Andy had been head of Global Studios for nineteen years now, and had outlasted all the other heads at rival studios. He was admired and respected and did his job well.

By the time Andy was in his early forties, he was as powerful as any studio head in the business, and little by little he had outstripped them. The qualities he had inherited from his father set him apart from everyone else. Honest, straightforward, hardworking, he was considered a man of integrity and honor. Not only did he have a brilliant mind for the business, he backed it with unfailing honesty. He was a man to be trusted. He had watched others fall in the last nineteen years, but his position only became more solid. The business didn't corrupt him, nor did the vast amounts of money he dealt with, but eventually the volume of his work devoured him. He had grown up with strong family values, which never left him, but the life of a studio head left little or no time for a family or ordinary pursuits. He was always somewhere, checking a film on location, calming a major star who wanted to quit, or making a deal for a new movie. He was the ultimate peacemaker as well as dealmaker, and he had learned from his parents how to coexist with stars and their demands. He had grown up among the biggest stars in the business. Nothing daunted him or frightened him or stopped him.

At forty-five, he had been married for twenty-one years when his wife, Jean, told him she was divorcing him. There was no scandal involved. She told him simply that she had hardly seen him for the past seven years, since he had become a studio head, and it was only going to get worse. He knew she was right. Andy was too good at what he did and loved it too much. Global had tripled its profits in the seven years he'd been the CEO. Andy and Jean's daughter, Wendy, was in college, and he knew he had been an absentee husband and father for some very important years. He had missed every birthday and school event. Jean had had to be both mother and father to their daughter for all the times Andy hadn't been there. Jean went to most social events alone. He didn't have the time. He loved his wife and daughter, but he loved his job at least as much. He didn't fight the divorce and was extremely generous with Jean, and always spoke highly of her.

In the twelve years since their divorce, Jean had remarried a cardiac surgeon, lived a suburban life in Cleveland, and was extremely happy. Wendy had married in the meantime too. She had always stayed as far as she could get from the Hollywood world. She had seen it devour her father's personal life and destroy her parents' marriage. She was happily married at thirty-two with a son and a daughter, Jamie and Lizzie, and lived in Greenwich, Connecticut. She was married to a book publisher and was an editor herself. Andy had dinner with them when he had business in New York, but readily admitted he saw too little of them. Wendy didn't hold it against him. She understood who he was. He had sacrificed his personal life for his success. She had never asked him if he thought it was worth it. She assumed he thought it was. It was the life he had chosen, and he seemed to have no regrets.

Andy had never remarried after the divorce. He had had a series of relatively long-term girlfriends, in Hollywood terms. His relationships lasted for two or three years, often with a major star. He always had a famous actress on his arm, reminiscent of his own mother. Both of his parents had died by then, and his daughter and grandchildren were his only living relatives. Wendy meant the world to him, no matter how little he saw her, and so did her children. He called her frequently and kept current with her life, but he had little time to see her. He knew she understood the demands of his job, and what it meant to him. He **was** the job by now. It was part of him, like a vital organ.

His current girlfriend was Alana Beal, a truly talented actress who had done several movies with his studio since she had come from England to LA. She was a tall, cool beauty in her forties with stunningly glamorous looks, and she was an intelligent woman. He enjoyed talking to her. He had never abused the perks of his job or his position by seducing young actresses. He was an intelligent man of substance and all the women who had dated him spoke well of him. The relationships always ended because, as generous and kind as he was, he had no intention of marrying again and said so right from the beginning. Sooner or later the women he went out with realized that he meant it, and if they had marriage in mind, they moved on, usually at about the right time. Eventually another woman well-known in some field, usually movies, would take her place. The system worked well for him, and the relationships had usually reached their expiration dates by the time they ended.

Andy Westfield was supremely comfortable in his professional life, in the role of studio head, which was a dream come true for him. He had been one of the most important men in the film industry for exactly one third of his life, nineteen years out of fifty-seven. He had hit his stride and was sailing along. Being a man of immense power was second nature now, and he never abused it. He didn't need to, and it wasn't his style. He didn't need to show off. He was comfortable with who he was. He never wasted his time looking far to the future. He lived in the now. His future was secure. He didn't need to worry about it. He had made an immense amount of money and invested it well, unlike his parents, who had spent all of theirs by the time they died.

He assumed he would stay where he was until he grew old, and would retire one day. He had improved Global's profits so astronomically that AMCO, their parent company, had no complaints, and there was no reason that would change. AMCO had made numerous acquisitions in the past two decades, and loved the excitement and glamour of owning a major film studio. Andy had never let the company down. He had become a Hollywood legend himself. With Andy running Global, it was a lovefest all around. Tony Bogart, the CEO of AMCO, liked to say they had gotten their money's worth when they hired Andy.

*   *   *

Frances, Andy's assistant of fifteen years, came into his office through a side door from her own. She had an office right next to his, so she could be at his beck and call constantly. She handled everything for him, including his social engagements. She had a respectful, friendly manner. She had just turned forty, and was twenty-five when she had started working for him. Being his assistant was a vocation almost like a religious calling to her. She worshipped him and lived to make life easier for him in every possible way. She was consummately discreet and reliable, and above all a trustworthy and kind person. She knew everything about his life, and got him out of things he didn't want to do with such grace that no one knew that the excuse wasn't real. Her friends accused her of being in love with him, which she didn't entirely deny, but she knew that nothing would ever come of it. There had never been even a hint of anything inappropriate from him. He was a very proper, respectful man, and she was well paid to do her job. She loved it, and keeping him punctual and organized.

"Just a reminder, Andy. You have to leave in ten minutes. You're picking up Ms. Beal at four-thirty. Red carpet starts at five. And you should leave your house at four. I gave you an hour in the schedule to dress. Julian will be downstairs in ten minutes to take you home." Julian had been with him for a year. His drivers never stayed long. They were mostly out-of-work actors hoping to be discovered by him, which had never happened.

"Alana will be late anyway. I can have a drink at her place while I wait. She doesn't have you to organize her. Her assistant is more disorganized than she is." He grinned at Frances, who had red hair and freckles and looked like the girl next door, even at forty. She had no film aspirations. She'd gone to Princeton, and had taken the job for a summer and stayed, once Andy discovered how incredibly organized she was. She was from the East, and her family could never understand why she had taken a job as a personal assistant and stayed in it.

She was conservative in her dress, as he was, and wore businesslike suits in dark colors to the office. Andy always wore a suit and tie to work. His daughter Wendy teased him about being "old school," but he was respectful of his job and the people he saw every day. And Frances was too. Dressing the part came with the job, for both of them. Most of Andy's counterparts wore jeans and even T-shirts to the office now, and sneakers, and their assistants looked like they were going to the beach. There was no question that Andy Westfield was a very important man. You could tell just by looking at him.

As she always did, Frances got him out the door on time. He had no appointments that afternoon. He took the private elevator down. Julian was waiting downstairs and took Andy to the house he'd bought in Bel-Air after the divorce. He had given Jean the house in Beverly Hills where Wendy had grown up, which Jean sold when she remarried and moved to Cleveland. Andy's house in Bel-Air was enormous, with a gigantic pool and patio where he could easily give parties for a hundred, with magnificent, sculpted gardens. The interior was exquisite too, with museum-quality art and more of his parents' movie posters. His job had made him a rich man over the years, and he liked living well and the perks of his success. He had inherited very little from his parents except their Oscars, and the wonderful memories he had of them.

Andy had thoroughly enjoyed his childhood. His parents had taken him everywhere with them. His father had made many of his films in Texas and Arizona, and his mother would take him to visit when they were on location. John had taught Andy to ride when he was four, and he was an excellent rider. He had so many warm memories of them, especially fishing with his father, who loved to fish. They had visited his mother's hometown in Sweden, where she was revered. He had ridden in several parades with his father when he was a little boy, riding his own horse. And they had gone to rodeos. They had visited John's parents in Montana several times before they died. Considering the possibilities in Hollywood, Andy had lived a relatively healthy life, with loving parents.

At times, he regretted not having had more time

to spend with Wendy. She didn't have the rich history of memories that he was lucky enough to have, and he was grateful that she never seemed to hold it against him. Jean had wanted more children, but as an only child, he didn't, and they both realized later that it was just as well. He would have had even less time to devote to more children. Andy's father had taught him so many things that he'd never had time to share with Wendy. Andy and Jean lived in a different, faster-moving world. There had been more time, even with movie star parents, when Andy was a boy. The years had flown by until Wendy left for college, and he realized at her high school graduation, and even more so when she graduated from Columbia, that he had missed it all.

She stayed in New York after college and never moved back to LA. Then, two years later, he was walking her down the aisle when she married Peter Jensen. Andy's family life had been in fast-forward for as long as he could remember. For twelve years now since his divorce, he had lived the life of a bachelor in his spectacular home. It was much bigger than he needed, but it went with his image and stature as a studio head, and it was an ideal place to entertain, which he didn't have time to do either. He hadn't given a party in several years. And he almost never saw old friends. His work dinners came first.

Frances kept his house efficiently staffed. Many

of the people she had hired had been there since he bought the house. He had a butler, Timothy, who was English, several people who cleaned the house, a fleet of gardeners. He didn't keep a cook, because his schedule was erratic and he went out a lot, or ordered in from his favorite restaurants when he wanted to eat at home. The housekeeper cooked for the staff.

His dinner jacket had been laid out by the butler, the night of the Academy Awards. He helped Andy dress and did his cufflinks and impeccable bow tie for him.

Two of Global's recent movies had been nominated.

Alana, Andy's current girlfriend, hadn't been nominated this time and had never won an Oscar. His parents' Oscars were displayed in shadow boxes along one wall in the library. Alana was an exceptionally good actress. She and Andy didn't live together but saw each other three or four times a week, including the weekends they spent together when he had time. This would be her third time going to the Academy Awards with him.

Wendy had met Alana a few times but wasn't close to her. She knew her father's women didn't last, so she didn't make any effort to spend time with them. He came alone when he visited Wendy and Peter, and their son, Jamie, and daughter, Lizzie, in their home in Greenwich. Alana wasn't part of Andy's family life and didn't expect to be. She was divorced too, and had no children. Her career was the main focus of her life, just as his was.

Andy left on time and was at Alana's at precisely four-thirty. She lived in a small, elegant house in the Hollywood Hills. She usually stayed at his house when they were together. Andy looked impeccable, his blond hair graying slightly, his vibrant blue eyes, his face alive with interest in whatever he was doing or who he was talking to. His tuxedo had been made by his tailor in London. Every inch of him was perfection. He was as handsome as any actor, his face was lit from within with intelligence and experience, and there was an aura of power about him. It was easy to guess that he was an important man. Alana always dated powerful men or famous actors and had made a career of it.

She rushed into the living room where he was sipping a vodka martini. She was breathless and beautiful. It was five to five, and she was almost half an hour late. She was a tall, very slim woman in her forties, with full breasts pouring out of a white dress that looked like it was wallpapered to her and was vintage Chanel couture. She had borrowed it for the evening, as she did everything she wore to major events. It had been flown in from Paris and fitted to her. She was wearing long diamond earrings that Andy had given her on their first anniversary, with a diamond necklace she had borrowed from Van Cleef. Alana knew just how to do red carpet events, especially the Academy Awards. She and Andy went to the Golden Globe Awards every year too.

"Wow, Ms. Beal!" Andy said, beaming at her. "**You** are a vision! They should give you an Oscar just for the dress." He looked at her appreciatively and she smiled at the compliment and pirouetted for him. Her blond hair was in a sleek French twist and all the diamonds sparkled. A team of makeup artists, hairdressers, and a manicurist had just left.

"They took the dress out of the Chanel exhibit for me. Elizabeth Taylor owned the necklace. Richard Burton gave it to her," she said proudly. The trappings of stardom were all-important to her.

"He would have given you a bigger one," Andy said, smiling as he approached to kiss her. He always enjoyed her company. He wasn't madly in love with her, but they were comfortable with each other, which was all he wanted. She was a bright, interesting woman and a good actress, and he didn't have any illusions about the fact that if he wasn't who he was, she wouldn't have been dating him. But the arrangement worked for both of them, and they were a familiar pair in Hollywood. She loved being in the press with Andy, and he didn't mind. He was used to it, and it was important to Alana. He had never found the kind of relationship his parents had, even with Jean when he was married to her. His parents' relationship really was a love match, but he guessed that his father had been a more attentive husband and had had more time to spend with his wife.

Andy remembered distinctly how his mother's face had lit up when his father walked into the room, and the slow smile on his father's handsome face when he put his arms around his beautiful wife. It had embarrassed Andy as a child, but now he remembered it fondly. He and Jean had always been more matter-of-fact with each other, and playful when they were younger. They had married soon after college. But Jean didn't have a romantic nature, and Andy was shy when he was young.

They became more like friends than lovers as time went on, particularly when he got busy with a big job. Their friendship had carried them through the years, but not all the way to the end. She had admitted to him when they divorced that she had been lonely married to him. Andy thought Jean's new husband was intelligent but dull, although he was supposedly a talented surgeon at the Cleveland Clinic and people came from all over the world to be operated on by him. But Jean said they did everything together when he wasn't working, which was something she and Andy had never done, and she had had no interest in the glamorous side of Andy's life.

Jean had hated going to the Academy Awards and having attention focused on her and Andy. She always felt like she'd worn the wrong dress and felt like a drudge compared to the movie stars. They were impossible for a normal human to compete with. Andy was always very polite and told her she looked lovely, but there was no excitement in his eyes when he said it to her, or in hers. They had fallen out of love with each other and hadn't noticed, while he was running the studio and she was driving Wendy to soccer games and ballet classes. Over the years she had become a soccer mom, and he was surrounded daily by gorgeous movie stars. He had never cheated on her while they were married, but in the last few years of their marriage they hardly ever made love anymore. They had outgrown each other.

The women he dated after the divorce were almost always movie stars. They were readily at hand, and eager to be seen with him. It was easy for him. Alana was a prime example of that. Such women fed his ego, but never touched his heart. He didn't expect to fall in love again, and he hadn't. But it was important to him to be with a woman he could talk to. He had no interest in ingénues and starlets. They looked like paper dolls to him. Alana was intelligent, even if she was ambitious, and constantly aware of what was good for her career. But he was never bored or embarrassed to be with her. She was ladylike, and he enjoyed being with her, whatever her motives. She wasn't interested in marriage either. Just in furthering her career.

When Andy and Alana got to the red carpet, the press rushed toward them, and Alana looked dazzling in the white gown, with the diamonds sparkling on her neck and ears. She posed for the cameras and she and Andy stopped several times, and once inside, the television cameras focused on them constantly. Andy took it in stride. He had lived with it all his life. It was all familiar territory to him.

Both of Global's films won, one for best picture, the other for best actress, and Andy was pleased. He had expected them to win, but it was always gratifying and never got old. He was proud of the studio, and to be the head after all these years.

He and Alana went on to the two most important after-parties when the ceremony was over, and the press crowded them again on the way out. Alana was ready for them, her hand tucked in Andy's arm as they made their way through the crowd, and they talked to an endless stream of people at the parties. Andy was tired of it by the time they got to the second one, but he knew how much Alana enjoyed it, so they stayed, and he chatted with Phil Lieber, an important producer he knew, while Alana stopped for a minute to talk to a friend.

"What do you think of the rumors about AMCO?" Phil Lieber asked him, with a martini in his hand. Andy was tired of talking and drinking by then and looked unimpressed by the question.

"I keep hearing they're going to sell Global." It was the kind of thing people said, but it never went far. There was no substance to it, just gossip.

"Nothing new there, Phil. Every time there's a blip in the stock market, someone says they're going to sell. AMCO loves being in the movie business. There have been rumors like that as long as I've been at Global." Andy was visibly bored by the conversation. Lieber was a scaremonger, and Alana caught the tail end of the conversation when she got back.

She brought it up to Andy on the way home in the car. Andy was dropping her off at her place. It was late. He had an early meeting the next morning, and she never stayed with him after the Awards. She would want to gossip on the phone with all her friends the next morning, and he would be in his office long before she woke up.

"What was that Phil Lieber was saying about AMCO selling Global? Someone else said it to me last week. It sounded crazy to me, but is it true?" She looked worried, and she frowned as much as her latest Botox shot would allow.

"I hear that stuff all the time. They're not selling. I doubt they ever will. They have too much fun being in the movie business. And we make them a ton of money," he said confidently.

"Good, I'm glad you're not worried."

"No, I'm not. Thank you for joining me tonight,"

he said, as his Bentley came to a stop in front of her house.

"I loved it. I always do, thank you for taking me," she said, and kissed him lightly on the lips. "Do you want to come in?"

"I'd love to, but I'm dead. And I've got a breakfast meeting tomorrow at the crack of dawn." She wasn't bothered by his refusing. She hadn't expected him to spend the night, or even come in for a while. They were both tired, but she thought it best to ask. "I'll see you on Saturday," he said, and kissed her just before she got out, and then he walked her properly to her door and saw her in.

He was back in the car two minutes later, thinking about Global's two films that had won. He was always pleased at their wins. They had at least one Oscar-winning film every year, or several, for best actor or actress or director or best picture. The sweet smell of success was so familiar to him now. He didn't take it for granted, but he was accustomed to it and considered it the norm.

The driver took him home, and when Andy crossed the patio, he noticed how beautiful the pool was, all lit up. It was a balmy night with a star-filled sky, and he sat down for a minute, just to enjoy it. He sat back in one of the lounge chairs and looked up and smiled. He remembered nights when he had gone camping with his father in Wyoming and Montana and how close the stars had seemed, and how full of falling stars the sky was. The memory of it still warmed his heart. As he looked around at his home, he realized again that he was a lucky man, and all was well in his world. He couldn't imagine a better life than the one he had.

Chapter 2

Andy's breakfast meeting the next day was with Tony Bogart, the CEO of AMCO, Global's parent company. Tony had been in the job even longer than Andy had been in his, and had been the one to hire Andy nineteen years before. They knew each other well, and were cordial but had never been close friends. Tony was sixty-four now, approaching retirement, seven years older than Andy, and had been at AMCO for twenty-five years. He had clawed his way to the top. There had been many broken men and careers left in his wake. Anyone foolish enough to challenge Tony's absolute power or put him at risk in any way was sure to come to a bad end. Andy had never put him in that position. It wasn't in his nature, and he didn't need to. Andy ran a fiefdom all his own, did it brilliantly with concrete results that AMCO could bank, and had always maneuvered carefully around Tony, knowing to pay homage to his ego and his rank. It didn't take much to keep Tony happy, and to this day he took full credit for having handpicked Andy for the job. It had been a wise choice that had paid off for them all.

The two men couldn't have been more different. Andy was quiet and discreet, much like his genuinely masculine father, with the best traits of his kind, while Tony was consumed with ambition and always somewhat paranoid, watching his back. When in doubt, he attacked, and he had injured enough people in his career to have justifiable concerns that someone might be after him, for either revenge or his job. Andy wasn't his enemy, so he knew he was safe with Tony. Tony was insatiable in his pursuit of power and had a weakness for young women. He had married twice during Andy's tenure in his job. Andy had gone to both weddings. Tony was recently divorced and dating another twenty-five-year-old. She was a trade show model he had met through an escort service. Under the slick surface and the expensive Italian suits, there was something sleazy about Tony that Andy had never liked, but he never let it show.

They met at the Polo Lounge. Tony ordered a hearty breakfast, and congratulated Andy on his wins the night before at the Academy Awards. Andy had final say on every movie that Global produced, and an infallible instinct for success.

"You knock one out of the park every time," Tony said admiringly. "You have the best nose in the business for talent and the pictures that will work. The boys upstairs at AMCO will be happy," he added, looking relaxed. They had breakfast once a month to bring each other up to date on any news they wanted to keep confidential and not put in emails. Tony was particularly careful about not leaving a trail of his communications. AMCO had survived several big lawsuits, with enormous settlements over the years, and he had learned the lesson the hard way. So far, Andy had never had anything to hide, which was a surprisingly clean record in the film industry. He set a strong example of principled transactions and honorable dealings, even more rare in their business.

"I learned it from my dad," Andy said modestly. "My father had an incredible eye for great talent," and had discovered many young actors who went on to become big stars, and who always credited John Westfield for giving them the chance.

Andy only had cereal and toast, and they were both drinking their coffee when Tony leaned back in his chair, looking relaxed, and brought up the real reason for their breakfast this time. "I'm sure you've started hearing some of the rumors around town. Gossip flies around Hollywood faster than fires in Malibu," he said, while Andy waited for him to deny them, as he had before. Rumors about

AMCO and Global weren't new to either of them. AMCO was an enormous entity with a voracious appetite, and Global had become the most successful studio in the business, thanks to Andy, so the gossip mill worked overtime about them. Tony leaned forward in his seat, and spoke conspiratorially to Andy, so not even a waiter could hear them. The Polo Lounge was full of the most important players on the Hollywood scene, in music, in film, actors, producers, studio executives. Big business and delicate negotiations were conducted in that room.

"I never pay attention to the rumors," Andy said, looking relaxed. "If they're true, we will find out soon enough, and most of the time they're not, about Global anyway. We have no secrets."

"That's not entirely true," Tony said, in a voice barely louder than a whisper, "this time anyway. I wanted to give you a heads-up. AMCO has made some big decisions. Global is in great shape, thanks to you, but some of our other companies are suffering from the times. Globalization and technology have knocked the bottom out of some of our investments. We want fresh blood and an influx of money. We weren't considering Global for how to get it, but FAQTS made us an incredible offer. Apparently, they've had their eye on Global for a long time. It's a personal interest. FAQTS is still a privately held company, and it's huge now. They own some of the biggest streaming services, and they want to expand into the moviemaking business. We made a decision. We're going to sell. It comes as a surprise to me too, but it makes sense for AMCO financially. They're paying us billions. Your job is secure, of course. It's a new business for FAQTS, and you're the obvious one to run it. Some heads may roll at the lower end, but you're safe at the top. You have nothing to worry about. But we thought you should know. We've been in secret talks with them for months, and the numbers have lined up right for us, so it's a go. We're working out the fine points now, and we'll bring you into it as soon as the deal is signed, so you can meet everyone. They're very excited about you, Andy. It's all still confidential, of course, so you can't talk about it, but I wanted to let you know. It's not just gossip this time, it's real."

Tony looked satisfied as he sat back in his chair again, and Andy looked shocked for a minute. He wasn't expecting that. Not by a long shot. He had gotten his job nineteen years before, when AMCO had bought Global Studios and fired the previous studio head. Traditionally, a new owner made a clean sweep and fired the people who had been running a company they bought. It was how he had become studio head at thirty-eight, when Tony offered him the job. It wouldn't be surprising if a new owner did the same now and replaced him, but Tony was adamant that Andy had no cause for concern, and although Andy didn't like him, he believed him. Historically, Andy had been the best thing that had ever happened to Global. He had made it the success it was now.

Andy had no plans to retire at fifty-seven. He loved his job. He knew that Tony was planning to retire in the next year or two, saying he had had enough of corporate life. Andy wondered if that was true. What would Tony do with himself without being a key player in the power game? The young blondes he collected, or even a new wife, wouldn't be enough to entertain him. He had a yacht and a plane, and lived a high life. Andy couldn't see him being satisfied with chasing women and playing golf. But for now, Tony was still in the job, and the news he had just reported to Andy was major.

"I wasn't expecting that. I thought you were going to blow off the rumors. I thought they were just the usual bullshit. I denied them to Phil Lieber last night. I didn't think there was any truth to them."

"Well, keep denying them for now. We won't be ready to make the announcement for a few more weeks, maybe a month. We've agreed to the terms, but we haven't signed the final docs yet. And you know how that is. Some kink always comes up at the last minute that can screw the whole deal and needs to be ironed out. We don't want that to happen. AMCO wants the money, and it will be a record-breaking deal when FAQTS signs on the dotted line. You're part of industry history, Andy," Tony said, and patted him on the back, but Andy Westfield already was legendary and had been for nearly two decades. Being part of a multibillion-dollar deal would only add to that. "And remember, you're in good shape here. You have my personal guarantee of that." Tony paid the check then, on his AMCO credit card, and the breakfast meeting ended on the astounding news he had shared.

Julian was waiting outside for Andy in the company car, a Mercedes-Maybach that was even more expensive than the Bentley Julian had driven for him the night before, which Andy owned. He often preferred his own car to the larger, even showier car the studio provided for him. He was pensive on the way back to his office and had a lot to think about.

New ownership was likely to be complicated for a while. There would be a long period of adjustment while he and FAQTS got used to each other, while Andy learned what their vision was for the company. They weren't likely to just leave things as they were. He would have to discover the changes they wanted to make, and negotiate for the studio and convince FAQTS that he knew how things worked

best. It wouldn't be an easy time, and would inevitably require a major revamping of Global's sys-
tems, particularly since FAQTS was so high-tech.
A private owner could be much harder to deal with
than a corporate one, which was more impersonal.
Now he'd be dealing with the personality and
quirks and prejudices of an owner. It could play
to his advantage in the end, but would take finesse
and grace until he learned what a new owner expected of him. He was glad that Tony had warned
him so he could think about it and prepare, and he
was also grateful that Tony had reassured him that
his job was safe. It had never even occurred to him
that AMCO might sell Global Studios one day. It
was the farthest thing from his mind.

It pained Andy to realize that others wouldn't be
as secure, and he would inevitably have to let some
key people go when the new owners arrived. He
knew what that could do to people's lives, and it
would be a challenge to maintain morale during
the handover, with people panicked about losing
their jobs. He would have to stay close to his top
management to avoid mass panic in the ranks. It
was going to be an unsettling time, but at least he
had time to prepare for it now.

Andy thought of Global almost like a family, with
him as the patriarch at the top. He cared about
each and every one of his employees, all the way
down to the lowliest ones. There was no such thing
as "lowliest" to him. They all mattered to him, even

those he didn't know and had never met. They all had lives and dreams and families that depended on them. And for those he would have to let go, it would be life-changing for them. Maybe for the best in the end, if they found better jobs. It would be an art form to integrate new faces in with the old. He was going to suggest several retreats to HR, and training programs with games to facilitate the change. There was a lot to think about, not for himself, but for all the others. With more than a thousand employees, the ripples would be felt throughout the company, and he would have to keep the ship steady once the sale was announced. It would be huge news in the industry, and there would be the press to deal with too. Global's media and PR departments would be busy, keeping a positive spin on the change. Maybe it would be good news in the end. Maybe a fresh point of view would strengthen the studio even further. It was all he could hope for now, waiting for the news to become public. Tony had said in a few weeks or a month. Andy had some serious planning to do until then.

Andy was quiet in the elevator riding up to his office, his mind whirling with the news Tony had shared with him. He looked serious when he walked into the inner sanctum, after the receptionists greeted him when he walked by. Frances was putting messages on his desk when he came through the red doors. She turned to look at him with a smile and was surprised that he didn't look happier after the wins of the night before.

"Are you okay?" she asked cautiously. She thought he looked serious and perturbed.

"I'm fine." He smiled at her, always polite and personable, and professional in his demeanor, but she knew him well. Something seemed off to her. "Just a lot on my mind. I'm tired after last night. Wonderful news, though, and not surprising. They're both great pictures." He set down his briefcase, which she took and put away as he sat at his desk. He looked more stressed than tired, and she wondered if there had been a problem with Alana. She could be a diva at times, although he was patient with her too. He had an even, calm temperament, and was slow to anger, which his mother had always attributed to his father's Montana origins. His father had been good-natured too. His mother had a cheerful nature but could be high-strung at times. Andy was used to women who could be nervous and demanding, although his ex-wife had never been difficult. She had been easygoing, reasonable, and fair, even about their divorce, which was why they were still friends.

The women since her had been better looking but not as easy to get along with, but since he wasn't married to them, it rarely upset him. A little time and breathing space always calmed things down, and eventually a change of woman would be inevitable. After fifteen years, Frances was surprised that Alana had lasted this long, but Alana was careful with Andy and didn't make scenes with him as a rule, which wouldn't have gone over well. Frances had always liked Jean, with her calm, down-to-earth style, and very few of the women since her. Alana was always haughty and high-handed with Frances, with the arrogance of some stars, and made sure that Frances felt she was an inconsequential being in her life. Her only importance to Alana was as Andy's assistant, to help her get whatever she wanted. Frances hoped she'd like the next one better. Lately, she had a feeling it might not be too long a wait. Alana was getting increasingly pretentious and demanding. Andy had noticed it too, but he didn't want to deal with it yet. There were still things he enjoyed about her. And she was a good traveling companion. He liked going on trips with her.

Once Andy was settled at his desk, Frances reminded him that he was going to the Napa Valley the next day, with Alana, to stay at a newly redecorated hotel she wanted to see. They'd been to Napa before, and she loved the wine and the food. He was planning to use the company plane, as he always did, and land at a small airport not far from the hotel. Frances had arranged it with her usual efficiency and everything was in order. He saw she had written him a note about it as he went through his messages.

"Thank God you reminded me, I almost forgot." Tony Bogart's news had blown everything else out of Andy's head. "What time do we take off?"

"You have a ten-fifteen takeoff slot. Probably getting to the airport at nine-thirty or nine forty-five would do it. You won't have much luggage for the weekend." He smiled at what she said.

"I won't, but Alana will have four or five bags for costume changes. We'll get there at nine-thirty, just to be safe, so we don't miss our slot."

He sent Alana a text reminding her shortly after, and she responded at noon.

"Awfully early, no?" she said.

"It gives us time to check into the hotel and have a nice lunch," he responded. They had several favorite restaurants in the area. It was a trip they always enjoyed, and Napa would be lush and green by then, with vineyards everywhere that made it look like Italy. Alana had traveled to Europe with him too, and had been on many vacations with him, even on boats he had chartered in the Mediterranean. She always made the trips better and more fun for him. She was a good companion, whatever her motivations for being there. He wasn't entirely naïve about that, but it was a fair trade. Good company for him, and luxurious holidays for her, in the utmost luxury that was a given in his life, much of it due to his job, like the plane.

Throughout the day Andy's breakfast with Tony Bogart came to mind, and the shocking news Tony had shared. It raised many questions in Andy's mind about how best to handle it when the time came, and how to make the announcement with an appropriate mix of glitz and compassion so the new owners would feel they'd been given their due, and the worried employees of Global, and those who would lose their jobs, could face it with a minimum of panic. So many of them had families that depended on them. Andy never lost sight of that, particularly since his own job was secure. He could think of everyone else, as he always did.

He spent a quiet evening at home and picked Alana up at eight-thirty the next morning, to get to the airport on time to board the plane calmly without rushing.

As he had predicted, she had four valises and half a dozen garment bags with clothes she had borrowed for the weekend, most of them from Chanel. Her agent called the publicity offices of major designers, and either facilitated borrowing clothes for her or got her a big discount if she had to buy them. She was always elegantly and tastefully dressed and would have enhanced the image of any man she accompanied. She looked like a star. And Andy constantly looked like what he was, a very important man. Even in tennis shorts and a T-shirt, or jeans and a sweater, he had the aura of power about him. He had been at the top of his game for so long that it was part of him now, second nature. He got outstanding service everywhere he went. It never dawned on him that that might not be the case. Frances saw to it that every possible mishap was avoided, and he was shielded from any inconvenience. He got the best suites in every hotel, the smoothest reception and the best food at every restaurant, and service by the manager in every store, without even realizing it. The best of everything was reserved and set aside for him, and his every desire and need was anticipated before he could even think of it himself.

Even as a star, Andy's father hadn't received the kind of service he did. As a studio head, Andy was far more important and powerful than any star. He was the maker of stars, the ruler of his kingdom, whether he acknowledged it or not. Most of the time, he wasn't even aware of it. It was just how he lived, and what happened to him in the golden life he led. He had no real sense of how other people lived. He never thought about it. Everything in his life was designed for his comfort, with as little hassle and stress as possible. Frances played a big part in that, but people wanted to please him, and they wanted his business.

When he got to the plane, two stewards greeted him on the ground. The bags were whisked away. As soon as the plane took off, brunch was served, according to all Andy's preferences and Alana's. She thoroughly enjoyed being part of his rarefied world. She had dated other important men, though none quite as powerful as Andy, or as nice. Most men in shoes similar to his had a mean side to them, based on their own sense of importance. It was a personality Andy didn't have. He didn't need to make anyone else feel small in order to elevate himself. He was who he was, and had been in the job for nineteen years. His real power and influence in the industry were enough for him.

They landed in Napa at eleven-thirty and got to the hotel shortly after noon. The manager was waiting for them, with his assistant, and the best suite had been set aside and filled with flowers, with a bottle of champagne in an ice bucket. A waiter opened the bottle for Alana. Andy didn't want to drink that early in the day, but Alana never turned down champagne. Andy noticed that it was her favorite, Cristal.

They went to lunch at an excellent French restaurant, and for a drive afterward, enjoying the beauty of the valley. Frances had arranged for a car for them, a Range Rover. Alana thought a sports car would have been more fun, but Frances knew Andy would prefer an SUV or something similarly more discreet. Andy was never vulgar or showy. Alana had reminded Frances several times that Bentley made an SUV now, and was always slightly annoyed that she didn't take the hint. But Frances was there to serve Andy's needs, not Alana's, and always politely made that clear.

They went back to the hotel for a nap after their afternoon drive, and made love in the beautiful room with the view of the lush valley. He was an ardent lover, and they got along well in bed, which was part of her appeal to him. It was more athletic than romantic. Alana was a skilled lover, and so was Andy. He had learned some new things since the divorce. His lovemaking with Jean had been perfunctory in the last ten years of their marriage. Things had improved since then, although there was no deep emotion involved. Alana wasn't a warm, emotional woman, or a nurturer. She was more of a femme fatale, which suited her role in life as a movie star.

She looked suitably glamorous when they left for dinner. She was wearing beige suede slacks with a matching coat from Chanel, with elegant beige suede high-heeled boots and diamond studs in her ears that Andy had given her the year before for her birthday. People noticed Andy and Alana immediately when they walked into The French Laundry for dinner, and recognized her instantly. Several people came to their table to ask for her autograph. Alana loved it, and Andy watched her bask in her glory. He had lived with that all his life. People had asked his parents for autographs everywhere they went, even in gas stations, hospitals, or the post office. It was just part of their life, and he took it in stride. It was newer to Alana, who had only lived with it for some fifteen years.

They went to sleep with a fire in the fireplace in their room, and got up the next morning to go for a walk. Alana was wearing another Chanel outfit, in denim, with a denim bomber jacket, designer jeans, and matching shoes again. She looked like she had stepped out of a magazine. Andy wore plain jeans and his favorite old cowboy boots and a cashmere windbreaker that cost a fortune but didn't look it, which was more his style. He had brought an old Stetson cowboy hat too, and looked more like his father when he wore it. Alana could easily see the resemblance. He looked like one of his father's movie posters as they wandered through one of the small towns near the hotel.

All in all, it was a relaxing, easy weekend, and they made love again before they left the hotel. It had been a perfect break from their routine for both of them, and just what Andy needed to relax.

They landed back in LA at seven o'clock after a smooth flight, and got back to his house in Bel-Air at eight.

"Do you want to spend the night?" he asked

her gently, and she nodded with a smile. The easy weekend in Napa had brought them closer, as their trips together often did.

The housekeeper had dinner brought in for them from one of their favorite restaurants, and they swam in his pool afterward. It was refreshing and relaxing, and they lay on lounge chairs after their swim, talking softly. She was meeting her agent the next day to discuss a part she was hoping to get, and Andy had no major dramas to deal with at the moment, except the sale no one knew anything about yet. He wondered when the deal would be signed and the sale confirmed, and didn't say a word to Alana about it, as he had promised Tony Bogart.

They went to bed at midnight and watched a movie for a while until she fell asleep. He turned it off and watched her in his bed for a minute, exquisitely graceful and unnaturally beautiful. He wondered why he didn't love her. She was perfect in many ways, intelligent, interesting, well-traveled, glamorous, charming when she wanted to be. He enjoyed her company and was used to her, but there was a part of him she never reached, and he knew she never would. He was never sure how sincere she was, and no matter what happened, she never touched his heart. He strongly doubted that any woman ever would again. Other than his daughter and her children, the only thing he had ever truly loved for years was his job. He smiled, thinking about it, as he turned off the light and lay down next to Alana. Even if they weren't in love, it was nice having her in his bed. He didn't need more than that from her. Even she knew that his work was his first love, and the enormous power and influence he had was his drug of choice.

Chapter 3

For three weeks after Andy's breakfast meeting with Tony Bogart, things were strangely quiet. It reminded Andy of the proverbial calm before the storm. He had a sense of foreboding. If nothing else, there would be an explosion in the press once the news was announced that Global Studios had been sold, and it was going to turn the film industry upside down.

He called Tony twice, inquiring if there was news. Tony sounded in good spirits, almost jovial, and told him that things were moving forward, it just took time to get the contracts right and to tie up all the loose ends. Andy knew how long contracts could take, so he wasn't surprised. They took months sometimes on complicated deals where multiple studios or production companies were involved. With two mammoth participants like AMCO and FAQTS, the contracts would be inordinately complex. According to Tony, there were sixteen attorneys working on it. Tony assured Andy again that he would call him as soon as there was news.

Andy went away with Alana on the weekends, to help pass the time. She had just agreed to do a new film, and had a starring role, so she was in good spirits. They went to Palm Springs for a weekend, where he played golf and tennis. Frances found a house with a pool in Malibu for them, on a gloriously sunny late March weekend. They lay in the sun together, with Alana under an enormous, glamorous sunhat. They walked on the beach. They hated to leave on Sunday night, and it made Andy almost want to buy a house in Malibu. He never had before because his own house was so comfortable, but a weekend at the beach had done them both good. It was the most romantic weekend he had spent with Alana in three years.

When he got home that night, he remembered the changes that were coming. He had almost forgotten about it all weekend. He was sorry to see Alana leave on Sunday night, but she had to go home. Her new trainer was coming to her house at 6 A.M. She was getting ready for the movie, and wanted to get in top shape for the part. There were several nude scenes in it, and she didn't like using a body double for them. She was proud of her body. She stayed in exceptionally good shape, which Andy liked. He was fit and athletic too.

Andy was up early the next morning and got to the office at eight-thirty. He was surprised to see Tony Bogart waiting in his office when he walked in, talking on his phone. He ended the call when Andy arrived, and was hale and hearty. He seemed in a very good mood and announced to Andy that the deal between AMCO and FAQTS had been signed at midnight on Friday night. He said he hadn't wanted to bother Andy over the weekend and had waited until Monday morning to tell him. Andy was relieved to hear it, but wished he'd told him before the weekend, as it would have been nice and a relief to have been advised that the deal had closed.

"We're sending out a press release at noon," Tony told him, and Andy saw something strange in his eyes. He wasn't sure what it was, but it felt almost as though he was lording the deal over Andy, as if it were some kind of victory for him, which Andy didn't understand. The two men weren't competing with each other, or they weren't supposed to be. Tony worked for AMCO, so with the sale of Global Studios, he would no longer be involved. And Andy was well aware that if Tony had managed the sale well, he would be given a huge bonus, so it was a win for him. It was the size of the deal that was a victory for Tony and would make news, since he had been part of the negotiation.

"There have been some changes in the initial structuring of the deal," Tony said, sitting comfortably in one of the chairs in Andy's office. Andy sat down across from him.

"What kind of changes?" Andy asked.

"It was a surprise for me too," Tony said innocently. "It was a deal-breaker for them. We tried to fight it, but we couldn't. The new owner's son has been running a TV network for ten years, very successfully I might add. The son wants to get into movies now. I think his father bought Global for him, and the profit we make, of course." Tony's face grew serious, his eyes steely, and Andy's heart skipped a beat. "He wants your seat, Andy. He's going to be the new CEO. I didn't realize that was going to be part of the deal, none of us did. It was the sticking point and why it took us so long to sign, and giving him that was the only way the deal would close. It was a deal-breaker for them. We had no choice."

"What do you mean?" Andy said to him, feeling as though suddenly Tony was speaking to him in Chinese.

"The son of the chairman of FAQTS wants your job. You know how these things go. You came in the last time Global sold."

"You mean I'm out?" Andy looked stunned. He wasn't clear if they were shuffling him into another job, or he'd just been fired.

"I'm afraid so. I'm sorry, Andy. I thought you were safe, but we never are." As he said it, Andy saw the red doors to his office open and two of the familiar security men walked in. They didn't smile this time. They stood quietly by the doors, as Andy looked from them to Tony. He'd had no warning, no time to prepare, no explanation until now. "AMCO is going to take good care of you. We'll call your lawyer with the severance package this morning. We're giving you three years' salary, Andy. That's one hell of a lot of money." And so was Tony's bonus, Andy was sure. And he still had his job.

"And I'm fired. Just like that," Andy said in disbelief. Tony stood up then.

"You know how this works," he said coldly, and nodded at the two security guards. "We'll send you the contents of your desk, anything personal, and your art. This place won't look the same without it," he said, glancing around, and his eyes brushed past the wall of movie posters of Andy's parents. "The boys will escort you to your car."

"Can I say goodbye to my assistant?" Andy asked in a hoarse voice. His legs were shaking but it didn't show. Tony shook his head and didn't answer, nodded at the two men in black uniforms, and Andy followed them out of his office in a daze. The two girls at the desk stared at him in astonishment as he walked past them. The elevator was there seconds later and Andy walked into it with a security guard on either side, as though he were going to pull out a gun and start a mass murder in the office where he had worked and been revered for nineteen years. He left the building in a straight line, walking blindly. The Mercedes-Maybach was waiting right outside. One of the guards opened the door, and Andy got in without saying a word. Julian started the car, and Andy managed to say, "The house in Bel-Air." Julian glanced in the rearview mirror and saw Andy wipe a tear from his cheek as he stared out the window, while the familiar landscape rolled past. Andy felt as though he were in a foreign country, a place where he'd never been before. He almost felt as though he didn't speak the language. He tried to remember Tony's exact words, but he couldn't. All he could remember was two security guards walking into his office without knocking, and realizing what it meant. He almost had the feeling that Tony was happy about it, and thought Andy deserved it. He didn't believe now that AMCO had fought for him and his job. They had handed his seat to the new owner on a silver platter, along with Andy's head. Swift as a saber, it was done and he was gone. The gaping wound it left in his heart and soul was bleeding profusely. It was a death blow like no other.

He was surprised when they got to his house. It had taken no time at all, without traffic. He got out of the car and Julian got out and looked at him.

He stuck out a hand to shake Andy's. "It's been nice driving you, sir," he said. "They just let me go this morning. I guess they'll get you another driver. They told me to take the car back to the garage after I dropped you off." He didn't realize that Andy had been fired too, and what the security guard escort had meant. So, they had fired his driver, and were already reclaiming the car. Andy didn't care. He had his own cars. But he had no job now. He was unemployed, fired, out of work. He had been the head of a major studio an hour ago, and now he was no one. Andy shook Julian's hand, thanked him, and walked into his house.

Frances called him on his cell as soon as he got through the door. She was crying. "They just fired me. They wouldn't even let me say goodbye to you." She was sobbing.

"That's because I'm not there," he said somberly. "They fired me too."

"They **what**?"

"They sold the studio. The new owner's son got my job. I'm out." The reality began to sink in as he said the words, and he realized he had to call Wendy before she saw it on the news.

"How can they fire you?"

"They just did. That's how I got in nineteen years ago, when they bought the studio and fired the previous head. It's kind of like a domino game."

"I can't believe they did that to you." She sounded stricken.

"Neither can I. But they did. Security walked me out. How much severance did they give you?"

"Two weeks," she said in a small voice. She'd been saving for a vacation, now she'd need the money to pay her rent.

"You can work for me at the house if you want. I'll pay you more than they did. All hell is going to break loose here in about two hours when they announce it. You can man the phones and keep everyone off my back." It was going to be big news in Hollywood. The biggest in years, maybe ever.

"I'll be right over," she said, and hung up, as Andy walked into his study and sat down on the couch. He wanted to call Wendy. She picked up as soon as she saw it was her father.

"Hi, Dad, how are you? I was going to call you tonight. I haven't heard from you in a couple of weeks." He usually called her once a week, but he hadn't, concerned about the sale and not wanting to tell her about it. "Are you okay?"

He hesitated for a beat before he answered.

"I am, or I will be. I've got some weird news to tell you, Wen."

"Please don't tell me that you're getting married."

He laughed. "Not that bad. But bad enough. I just got fired. The studio was sold to a multibillion-dollar private company, and the new owner's son wanted my job." It was simple really, and easier to explain than to live with. "It happened about an hour ago, and they're sending out a release to the press at noon. I didn't want you to hear it on the news."

"Oh my God, Dad. I can't believe it. Did they give you any kind of warning or notice? Why didn't you tell me?"

"I just found out this morning. They told me about the sale three weeks ago, but they told me my job would be protected and I was safe. I guess they were wrong," he said, remembering that she had been thirteen years old when he got the job, and she'd wanted to know if she could go to movies now for free. Now she was thirty-two and had two young children of her own.

"Can you sue them? They can't just throw you out like that on a moment's notice."

"Yes, they can. That's how it's done. They'll compensate me in the severance package. I'm sure they'll take good care of me. They can afford to. But I'm out of a job, and head of studio jobs don't grow on trees. I may be out of work for a while," he said to her, or forever. With the limited number of studio jobs, and at fifty-seven, he wasn't even sure there would be another job before he hit retirement age. It was too much to think about right now.

"Can I tell Mom?"

"Sure. She'll hear it on the news anyway," Andy said. He felt as though he had climbed a mountain that morning and fallen off a cliff. "I'll call you soon," he promised Wendy, and got off the phone right after Frances arrived. She looked dazed, sheet-white under her freckles, and had mascara streaked down her cheeks. She burst into tears the minute she saw Andy, and he put his arms around her to console her.

"I can't believe they did this to you," she said, sobbing.

"To us," he reminded her. She was more worried about him than herself. He was the most powerful man in the film industry and they had fired him as brutally as they had her, with no notice. His financial situation wasn't precarious, but the blow to his ego and pride was enormous. His whole identity had been his job for nearly twenty years. He felt naked without it. Who was he now? He had no idea. He couldn't wrap his mind around it.

He walked to the bar in his office and poured himself a scotch on the rocks and offered Frances one. She declined. He took a long sip and thought about calling Alana and decided not to. She would hear it soon enough. The word would spread like wildfire. It was ten-thirty in the morning, and he had been out of a job for just over an hour by then. He felt like he was floating in space in a science fiction movie.

The phone rang and Frances answered it. It was Jean, calling from Cleveland. Wendy had just called her mother.

"I can't believe it. Those bastards. They're insane," Jean said to Andy. "Are you okay?" she asked him, sounding more like a sister or a mother than his ex-wife, but they were on good terms.

"I don't know. I think I am." It was kind of like

a car accident. He was still in shock. "I don't know what hit me yet. At my age, I may never get another job, not a big one like this."

"You will if you want one. You'll figure it out," she said gently, and felt sorry for him. "Let me know if I can do anything to help."

"Thanks, Jeanie. I'll be okay. Take care of our girl, you always do," he said gratefully. She always had, when he was too busy to, and thought he was so important as a studio head. Now that was gone. He had no idea what to do or be now, or even who he was. He felt as though he had been swept away by a tidal wave, and couldn't get his feet firmly on the ground again. Getting fired had knocked him for a loop, and he had the feeling that Tony had enjoyed it. Andy told himself he was being paranoid.

He had another drink at noon and turned on the TV to watch the news. And there it was, the second story in, that Andy Westfield, son of famous cowboy actor and director John Westfield, had been let go as head of Global Studios, which had just confirmed that they had been acquired by communications monolith FAQTS. The position of CEO had been filled by Jeff Latham, the new owner's son. The news report said that Westfield had not yet been reached for comment. As they said it, Frances looked out the window and saw all the TV network news trucks arriving and a flock of reporters stampeding across the lawn in front of Andy's house. They rang the front and back doorbells, and Frances instructed the staff not to answer and to pull the shades and draw the curtains. Within half an hour, they were under siege. The reporters were desperate to talk to Andy, and he flatly refused to comment. Frances tried telling them that he wasn't home but they didn't believe her, so they didn't move. Even if he was out, he would have to come home sooner or later.

Alana called Andy right after the noon news, and he took the call. She sounded chilly.

"Why didn't you tell me? You could have warned me." She sounded peeved, not sympathetic.

"I didn't know," he said.

"They didn't tell you?"

"No, they fired me flat when I got to work this morning. They told me about the sale in confidence a few weeks ago, but they said my job was secure. And this morning, they told me they had a change of plans. So that's it. I'm done." He wondered what her reaction would be. She sounded as stunned as he had been, and didn't know what to say.

"What are you going to do now?"

"I have no idea. I may not find another job, not soon anyway. Nineteen years, gone in an instant."

"I'm sorry," she said, but she didn't sound sympathetic. "Good luck, Andy," she said, which he knew was goodbye. She was not a woman of mystery and was blatantly transparent. He had served his purpose for three years, and they had had a good time, but he was of no use to her now without a studio to run. She hung up a minute later and he doubted he would hear from her again.

The phones went crazy after that, his cell, the house lines. People he didn't even remember meeting called him to say they were sorry, and pry about what he was going to do next. The envious and the jealous called, gloating, some of his oldest friends called, and more recent ones. Most of them were just curious and wanted to hear all the inside dirt. The people he respected didn't call and left him to reverberate and mourn in peace, out of compassion for him. Frances fielded all the calls, took messages, and kept a list of them, in case Andy wanted to call anyone back. He didn't.

He drank steadily through the day and she tried to get him to eat something, but he wouldn't. She hadn't either. The housekeeper made them sandwiches, which they didn't touch. He watched the news again at six. It was the top story by then, and they once again said that Andrew Westfield had been unavailable for comment all day. Tony had made a brief statement about the sale, and how pleased they were to be passing the torch to FAQTS and the Latham family, and AMCO was sure they would do a wonderful job. Tony made no mention of Andy. Nine hours after he had been fired, he was history. His nineteen-year reign was over. Long live the new king. Andy would be forgotten in the blink of an eye. And no one would give a damn about him in Hollywood. That was how it worked.

He remembered Tony saying to him that morning, "You know how it works." "Yes, I do," he said out loud to the TV, as Frances watched him. He didn't look as drunk as he was, but he staggered slightly as he crossed the room for another drink.

"You should have something to eat first," she told him gently. He'd been drinking scotch on the rocks all day.

"I'm not hungry."

"You're going to have an awful hangover tomorrow," she said softly.

"I'll take the day off work," he said, and laughed.

His lawyer had called during the afternoon, and it was the one call Andy took. Barry Weiss called to explain the severance package to him, and it was a good one. Three years' salary, which was astronomical, given what he was paid. He didn't have to work again if he didn't want to. He had a one-year noncompete, so even if he found a job as a studio head again, he couldn't begin working for another year. Barry said they had wanted a three-year noncompete, and he got them down to one. It was a generous package, but nothing they paid him could replace what he had lost. If he didn't take another job, or find one, he would have ended on a failure, getting fired. It was the nature of corporate life. And how could they repay him for the power he had lost, the respect, the image, the status, everything the job meant to him? Who was he now without that job? He was no one. They had stolen his identity from him. What would they pay him for that?

Alana didn't call him that night. He knew she wouldn't after her call to him that afternoon. She had nothing more to say to him. She hadn't shown up to comfort him. His assistant had.

Wendy called to make sure he was doing okay. Frances said he was, considering.

She stayed for as long as she thought was useful to him. The phones eventually slowed down, and the house staff could answer them. She promised to be back in the morning and told Andy to get some sleep.

After she left, he took the bottle of scotch out to the pool and sat down on a lounge chair. The news trucks were gone by then. It wasn't a story worth staying up all night for. It was Hollywood gossip and a business story. No one had killed or shot anyone. No one had taken a drug overdose. There were no bodies. There was just Andy sitting by the pool, drinking himself into oblivion so he didn't have to think. Nothing like it had ever happened to his father. He'd made cowboy movies into his seventies, and when the parts slowed down, he turned to directing. He'd never been fired from anywhere, nor had Andy until now. This was a first for him. The ultimate humiliation at fifty-seven. He was a man without a job now. It was like being a man

without a face, or a heart. He felt like he was bleeding to death.

He continued to drink in the lounge chair by the
pool, long after Frances left. He had left his cellphone in the house so no one could reach him.
There was no one he wanted to talk to. He just
wanted to be alone with his bottle of scotch. He
was still wearing his suit and tie, the one he had
been fired in.

He lay there staring at the pool and looking up
at the sky, until the bottle slipped from his hand
onto the cement, and he finally passed out. It had
been the worst day of his life.

Chapter 4

The day after he was fired was only slightly better than the day before. Andy woke up at six in the morning in the lounge chair at the pool. He had spilled some of the scotch on his tie and stained it. He sat up slowly, feeling as though his head was going to fall off, and walked back into the house. He lay down on his bed for another hour, and then he got up and showered. For the first time in years, he didn't bother to shave. He was drinking coffee and eating a piece of toast when Frances showed up at eight o'clock.

"How are you feeling?" she asked him, looking concerned.

"Probably about the way I look, like I drank a bottle of scotch yesterday." He smiled ironically and put down the paper that he had been reading. The story of his being fired, along with a list of all his victories in the past nineteen years, was in the business section of the **Los Angeles Times.** "Are the jackals still outside?" he asked Frances, referring to the news trucks. She nodded.

"But fewer than yesterday. They'll be on to some other story in a day or two. They won't hang around forever if you don't talk to them."

"I'm not planning to," he assured her. He felt like a prisoner in his own home, and a stranger in his life.

Wendy called him a little while later. The story was in **The New York Times** too. Not only was being fired humiliating, but it was a totally public event. All the major newspapers had run it. Andy couldn't imagine walking down the street without wanting to hide.

"Maybe I should grow a beard or wear a mask," he said to Frances, trying to make light of it, but there was nothing amusing about it. There was no part of what had happened that felt okay to him. He hadn't done anything to deserve it, and the **LA Times** commented that he had done an outstanding job for two decades and the new studio head would have a hard time filling his shoes.

The news trucks came back for two more days, and then finally gave up. By the end of the week, the last of the reporters and paparazzi were gone. People were still calling constantly, wanting comments from him, or to know the gory details, and how he felt about it.

Wendy was calling every day to check in and

invited him to Greenwich to stay with them for a week or two to get out of the house. She didn't say it to Andy, but she told her husband she thought her father should retire, and live a life for a change, instead of being devoured by his work. But the film industry was his life, and she couldn't imagine him doing anything else, or just playing golf for the next thirty years.

He was still young at fifty-seven, and it seemed inevitable that he would go back into the movie business at some point, but doing what? There were only so many studios left. Many of them had merged years before into big conglomerates, or were owned by major corporations like Global had been. There were only so many heads, and no vacancies available. He might have a long wait, or not get another job as a studio head during his productive years. Andy had been thinking of that too, and his spirits were in the tank. He told Wendy he would rather visit her after he bounced back, and he had no idea when he would. He sounded very down to her.

A week later, he still hadn't left the house, and Frances noticed that he was still drinking a lot. By the time she left at the end of the day, he always seemed drunk to her. She had never seen him that way, it had never happened before. He didn't want to go to any restaurants to eat, because everyone knew him, and he didn't want to be seen in public. He had nothing to say to anyone, and he didn't

want their sympathy, most of which was false anyway. There were plenty of people who reveled in
others' misfortunes, and he didn't want to be the
object of their pity.

He fell asleep at the pool every night with a bottle next to him and woke up with it empty every
morning. He knew he was feeling sorry for himself and couldn't help it. He felt as if his life as he
knew it had ended. He thought of going to a head-
hunter, but that would be embarrassing too. He
didn't need a job for a paycheck. FAQTS had paid
him handsomely, with an additional bonus from
AMCO, to get rid of him. He had three years of a
huge salary coming to him in a lump sum within
thirty days of his being fired. And his investment
portfolio was healthy. He didn't need a job, but he
needed something to occupy him.

It made him feel sick when he saw his art being
returned, and all the posters of his parents. It made
it all seem so final. The contents of his desk arrived in four boxes, which Frances unpacked and
put away. He found places for some of the art and
the posters of his parents and hung them himself,
to keep busy.

Two weeks to the day after he'd been fired, he
still couldn't believe the word applied to him and
was part of his life now. He woke up at the pool
again with another brutal hangover, and walked
into his study, where Frances was sorting through
bank statements, bills, and correspondence, which

she normally handled for him. He looked at her in desperation. He glanced at another list of messages for calls he wouldn't answer, and emails he didn't want to read, and said to her in a low growl, "Get me out of here." For a minute, she thought it was good news.

"You mean the house? Do you want your car brought around?" One of the men he employed at the house could drive for him, or he could drive himself. He hadn't left the house in Bel-Air in two weeks. The weather had gotten warm. It was April. She didn't know where he wanted to go, but it didn't matter. "Do you want the Range Rover?"

"No, I mean away from here. Venezuela, Guatemala, Peru, Tahiti, Samoa, the Galápagos, somewhere where no one knows me and doesn't give a damn if I'm unemployed." The word tasted like ashes.

"Are you serious?" She looked startled and didn't know if he meant it. He wasn't usually an exotic traveler. He went to places like Cannes, Paris, London, Berlin, for film festivals or premieres of Global's movies. Everything he did was work-related, or used to be.

"No, not those places. But I want to go somewhere away from here. Maybe for a few months until I feel like myself again and can go to the Polo Lounge for lunch without wanting to hide under the table."

"People will forget what happened eventually," she said, to encourage him, but they both knew

it wasn't true. They would tell the story of his getting fired forever, and whatever sidebar they could
add to it, which was why he was staying out of
sight, so there were none. He didn't want photos
of him going around town, doing mundane things,
or buying lunch. He had nothing else to do now.
He had no interests or hobbies, just his job. And
he didn't have that anymore. Work was fun to him.
Time off never had been.

"Maybe someplace civilized," he said thoughtfully, "out in the country somewhere. France is too
romantic and will depress me, and I don't want
to sit in some drafty chateau. It's too late in the
season to ski in Switzerland. I'll get fat on pasta in
Italy. And I don't speak the language in Germany,
France, Italy, or Spain. Maybe England." He looked
hopeful as he said it.

"Where in England?"

"I don't care, just so it's some small town in the
country where no one will know me. Or a beach
town, maybe something on the sea. Even Ireland,
but it rains a lot there. Just get me out of LA."

"I'll see what I can find," Frances said, and went
to get her laptop.

It didn't make it any easier that Alana hadn't
called him since the day he got fired and wasn't
likely to call again. He didn't call her either. He
didn't want to. He had seen a picture in the papers
of her at a fancy gallery opening with a well-known
director. Alana always protected her career and her

future. Andy was no longer of use to her, and no longer had access to the company plane. She was after another big fish now. Andy knew her, and knew the game. He knew he'd never hear from her again. She was as merciless as AMCO. He didn't really miss her, but he felt the rejection acutely. She was another perk of his job that had vanished overnight. It was almost funny, but not quite. He knew that one day he might laugh at all of it, but not yet. He felt each loss like a body blow, and he knew he was on the ropes.

He wondered what his father would have told him to do. John Westfield had never lived with rejection, nor been fired. He had been a star to the end of his days. The public never tired of him—even now, years after his death, people still watched his movies. Andy loved them too, and his mother's. He had been proud of his parents, and they wouldn't have been proud of him now. He felt like a failure, even though it wasn't his fault he had been fired. He had just been a casualty of the corporate wars. He was collateral damage of a fast move in a billion-dollar deal. They had sacrificed him to close it and keep the buyer happy. It made him feel even more insignificant.

He felt out of control now, with no sense of direction, like a ship without a rudder or a car with no steering wheel and no brakes. He had lost control of his life, and knew he had to find it again. He couldn't stay like this forever. It was terrifying.

*   *   *

Frances worked on it for two whole days before
getting back to Andy. She looked on the internet for houses to rent, furnished and fully staffed,
available for a month or two, as she guessed that
that was what he needed before coming back to LA
to pick up the threads of his life again. After she
saw a house she liked on the internet, she called
the realtor offering it. Most of the houses evaporated into thin air or were unsuitable. Very few
seemed decent once she started asking questions
about how close the nearest village was, or if the
house had central heating. It would still be cold in
England in April, and many of the photographs
looked depressing. Or their idea of "fully staffed"
was a cleaning woman who came once a week, or
Andy would have to bring his own cooking pots
and linens.

Frances came back to him on the third day of
her research for him and was sorry she didn't have
more to offer. She had come across a fantastic villa
in the South of France, but it turned out there
had been a major robbery there with owners and
staff tied up and robbed, and the realtor suggested
armed guards for protection, so she ruled that out,
and a charming villa in Siena, which had recently
had a fire and was under repair. So she stuck with
England. The crop of available houses wasn't plen-
tiful there either. She had found a farm in Norfolk
which sounded too rustic to her, and Andy wasn't

famous for wanting to rough it. He was spoiled by the comforts of his own home and the kind of hotels he went to, like the Hôtel du Cap, in Cap d'Antibes, but the Cannes Film Festival was coming up in a month, and the hotel would be full of people he knew who would be well aware of his current circumstances. So that was definitely out.

There was a cottage in the Cotswolds which looked adorable, but it was tiny, with only one bedroom and no staff, which she knew wouldn't suit him. She found a castle in the north of England, in severe disrepair, with no central heating, that had recently been used to make a horror film. And there was a house in East Sussex, in a town called Winchelsea Beach, which seemed like the best possibility, just outside a tiny, antiquated beach town, built on the thirteenth-century remains of a medieval town, which had long since been forgotten. The beach town had a population of nine hundred and the inland part of it had fewer than six hundred inhabitants. Oddly, someone had remodeled one of the old houses near the beach and turned it into a very large, luxurious hideaway. It seemed totally out of place. The house was bigger than Andy needed and was surprisingly fancy given the location. The rooms were huge and handsomely decorated, and there were very elegant marble bathrooms and a high-tech, modern kitchen. The realtor said it was fully furnished, and there were a housekeeper and a maid. They didn't stay in the evenings and didn't live there, but the housekeeper might be willing to cook a meal occasionally. The house had been seized by a bank in foreclosure, and the bank wanted to sell it. But they were willing to rent it for six months, to defray the costs of running it, and Andy would have to agree to vacate the house at the end of the six-month period if they sold it. Frances couldn't imagine his wanting to stay away for that long, and thought the rental was too long, but she told him about it anyway. The house was on the coast, there was a beach nearby, and it was less than three hours from London by car if he wanted to go to the city when he felt better. And there was a train, which took less than two hours. There was a small harbor with fishing boats and small sailboats. And the beach was a mile and a half long. And when she inquired, the realtor said there was a doctor, a dentist, a hairdresser, two grocery stores, two pubs, a fish market, an inn, a post office, and a church in the area. There were some larger coastal towns nearby, but Winchelsea Beach was tiny. The swimming and wind surfing were supposedly excellent.

The house itself seemed incongruous. Everything in it looked expensive and luxurious, and a little showy, which made no sense in an old-fashioned beach town. Whoever had built it obviously couldn't afford it, since the bank had foreclosed. There were two cars in the garage that were in working order, an old Land Rover and a station wagon, that were part of the sale, along with all the furniture. From the photographs, it looked like the owners still lived there, and hadn't been able to take anything with them. Even the paintings on the walls were being sold, according to the realtor representing the bank. The rental price was higher than most of the other rentals, but still way below anything in LA or in the States, or in London.

"What don't you like about that one?" Andy asked her.

"The town is tiny and the house is too big for you. It's got five bedrooms, and servants' quarters on the top floor. They're being used for storage now, because the two women who work there don't live in. Oh, and there's a groundskeeper. They said the garden is a little overgrown, they're leaving it alone for new owners. I just think it sounds big for you. You won't feel lost in a house that size?"

Andy smiled at her in answer. "I don't feel lost here, and it's a lot bigger than that place. It's actually kind of stylish-looking. I like it, and the art isn't bad. It does seem weird in that location, though. The owners must have overspent on it so they lost it." She told him the price of the rent, which seemed low to him. "I like that it's clean and modern, and not some crumbling old house with 'charm,' no heating, and terrible bathrooms. The bathrooms are nicer than mine here. They must have spent a fortune on them. I don't know, Frances. It looks okay to me. Six months is too long, but who knows, maybe I'll like it. I have nothing to do here. Maybe Wendy and the kids will want to come over when I feel better, or I can give it to them for a month or two, if I come back to LA early. It's the only decent house you showed me. When is it available?"

"Now. It's unoccupied. It's been vacant for three years. The bank hasn't been able to sell it. No one in the area wants a fancy house like that, and the realtor says the bank is asking too much, but they want to recoup what they lost on it, so now they're renting."

Andy looked at the pictures on her laptop again, and sighed. "Let's do it. I'll go crazy if I stay here, locked up in the house, dodging phone calls. I feel like I'm in jail, or under house arrest. It might be nice to have a beach nearby. Even if it's too cold to swim, I can walk on the beach. I don't suppose you want to come to England for six months to help me there?" he asked hopefully, and Frances looked instantly regretful.

"I'd love it, but my mom hasn't been well. She's seventy-five and she has MS and she falls down a lot. I moved her out from New York last year since she's alone now. I don't live with her, she has her own apartment, but I'll probably have to move her in with me soon, and I can't be that far away if anything happens. I check on her every day after work." He nodded. She was a good person and it made sense.

"I'll have to manage on my own. I want to cut way down on my correspondence. I just want to quietly disappear for a few months, till I figure out what to do with the rest of my life, or what I want to be when I grow up." He smiled at her. He was the most grown-up person, and the kindest, she'd ever known, and she was sad to see him leave now. "What are you going to do when I leave?" he asked her.

"I guess I have to look for a job. I'm going to be living on my vacation money starting next week," since they had only given her two weeks' severance, which seemed obscene to him, after fifteen years working for the company.

"I'm going to give you six months of the salary I'm paying you now, when I go." It was higher than the salary she'd been getting at Global as his assistant. "Don't wait for me to come back. I don't want you to miss opportunities if you find a good job. But this way you'll have enough money to wait until you find the right one. Don't sell yourself short. You're a marvel, and you deserve an employer who appreciates you. I'll give you a reference too. If you hate the job you find, you can always work for me when I come back. But I have no idea what I'm going to do, or when I'll come back to LA. Maybe I'll float around for a year. I just don't know. I feel as though I got torn up by the roots two weeks ago, and I'm blowing in the wind.

"I don't know what kind of job I'll take when I

come back. Maybe I'll do something completely crazy and work for a nonprofit foundation. I have no ideas at all so far, and I'm not so sure that at my age I'll find another big job in the film industry. And none of the studio heads are even close to stepping down. They're all doing a good job so they're not going to get fired. I don't see a future for me back in pictures, or any future at all for now."

She had already realized that and felt terrible for Andy. He was so painfully honest with her. All he could see ahead of him was a bottomless dark pit he was struggling every day not to fall into. And maybe the house in England at the seaside would stop his free fall. She hoped so. He was a good person and deserved a good life, doing something that made him happy. He certainly wasn't happy now, not by a long shot. She was beginning to think he was smart to leave town before he tried to reinvent himself when he got back.

She called the realtor back in East Sussex and organized renting the house. She wired the money to the bank the next day and got it all set up in twenty-four hours. All he had to do now was pack and leave. She booked a flight for him on Saturday night. Timothy, the butler, was going to drive him to the airport. Andy was taking a commercial flight for the first time in years. He smiled as he thought of it. He was a regular person now, and a damn lucky one. He knew full well that his financial circumstances were a blessing, and his severance had been a very good one. He didn't have to worry about where his next meal was coming from. He could do what he wanted and go where he pleased, he could run away to England to a house that looked more than comfortable. And maybe he'd find his way again, doing something he loved as much as his old job. He was leaving himself open to the winds of fortune, wherever they took him.

Andy told Wendy where he was going and how to reach him. She thought it was a good idea and said maybe she'd bring the kids to see him if he was still there in the summer. He said that for now he was going to be living day by day, and let himself drift for a while, to figure out where to be and what to do. He was open to all possibilities, and he was relieved to be leaving LA. He didn't want to run into any of the people he knew. Tony Bogart, who was a terrible memory now and had betrayed him by selling out to the new owners and sacrificing Andy, or Alana, with any one of her new boyfriends who would further her career now because Andy no longer could—he had ceased to exist for her the day he had lost his job. She wasn't who he wanted to be with anyway. She wasn't real. Most of the people he knew weren't. Maybe he hadn't been either. He questioned himself now on every subject, about who he had been, and who he should become. He hoped to find himself in England, either the old version or a new one.

The hardest person to say goodbye to on Friday

night was Frances, who had been so staunchly there for him for so many years when he was at the top, and especially now that he was at the bottom of his career, the low point of his life. She had been wonderful and supportive for the past two weeks, better than anyone else, and so had Wendy. He was lucky to have them both. He hugged Frances when she left the house on Friday night.

"Take care of you now. You've taken such good care of me." He had stopped drinking a bottle of scotch every night, passing out at the pool and waking up hung over every morning. He was still drinking, but not as much, and was planning to lead a healthier life in England than he had been recently in LA. He was going to try and eat right, exercise, and drink less. He had never drunk as much in his life as he had in the past two weeks.

Frances clung to him for a moment before she left. "Take care of yourself, and if it gets too lonely there or you hate the house, come home, and we'll figure out something else."

"Just be careful and find a good job where they treat you well and appreciate you." He had given her a glowing reference that morning to show potential employers.

After she left, the house was quiet. The staff were going to cover everything with dust covers while he was away. He stopped to look at one of the posters of his father and gazed earnestly into the eyes in the photo.

"I'll try to get back on the right path, Dad. I promise. I don't know what the hell happened here." It had all spun out of control so quickly. In minutes his career and his job had ended, and now he'd been washed up on shore and had to find his way again. Maybe he would in England, or after he got home, but he knew he had to find himself again. His father was smiling in the photo, and it felt like a blessing as Andy looked at him. Maybe it was all he needed to know, that his parents had taught him how to live right, and what mattered. He had to find those values again, and the path he'd been on. He had stumbled and fallen, and now he had to stand up again, and follow his own path with courage. Maybe it was all much simpler than he thought, and all he had to do was be a good person and believe in himself again. He suddenly realized as he stood there that he had lost a job, not himself.

Chapter 5

It was part of Andy's reeducation and entry back into the real world, traveling commercial again. Frances had bought him a first-class ticket, but other than bigger seats and a fancier meal, it wasn't much different from the rest of the plane. The security line had been endless at LAX, he had to take off his shoes and his belt and empty his pockets, go through the metal detector three times before he cleared, and then reclaim his belongings among pushing, shoving, harassed people at the other end, with security agents shouting, people complaining. They took him aside to go through his briefcase and put his computer through separately, which delayed him so he had to run for his plane. He had checked one suitcase, which had been an ordeal at the curb. For nineteen years, he had been spared the inconveniences of the real world and how stressful and complicated travel was now. He felt as though he had run a marathon by the time he got to his seat on the plane. He had a single seat at the window, sat down, and refused a glass of champagne. He wasn't in the mood for it. He was booked on a ten P.M. flight, had had to check in by eight for an international flight, and had left his house at seven. With the eight-hour time difference and ten hours in the air, he was due to arrive at Heathrow at four in the afternoon, and had a two-and-a-half-hour drive to Winchelsea after that.

He accepted a copy of the London **Financial Times** from a flight attendant and dozed off while he read it before takeoff. He was already exhausted before the plane even left the gate. The other passengers were busy settling in, putting their hand luggage in overhead racks, and several of them gratefully accepted the champagne to calm their nerves. There was no sign of the calm, easy departures he'd enjoyed for years on the company plane, where everything was taken care of for him. It was a wake-up call, being part of the mass of humanity again, even in the luxury of first class. He realized that he was lucky to even be able to afford that. The people in economy would sit bolt upright for the ten-hour flight to London, with no legroom for anyone as tall as he was, and only snacks for sale on the late flight. There was a curtain he could close around his area for privacy, and his seat reclined to a bed if he wanted to sleep. He could at least arrive rested and would be comfortable on the flight. He just wasn't alone, and was no more important than any other passenger.

He smiled thinking about it, and how symbolic it was of the changes in his life. He was no longer special or powerful. He no longer had thousands of employees, headwaiters in restaurants would no longer jump at the sound of his name. He had slipped many notches down in the world and was embarrassed to realize that it mattered to him, that he felt diminished by the status he had lost, and felt foolish for doing so. He felt humiliated and vulnerable, like a turtle without a shell now, a soldier without armor. There was nothing to protect him except himself, and he had to prove he was worthy of respect. It wasn't automatic at the mere mention of his name, or the studio he ran. He wondered if others felt as he did when they lost their jobs. He understood now how integral his job had been to his self-respect. What was there to respect now? Who was he? He was no one, headed for places where his name would mean even less. Doors wouldn't magically open for him, exceptions wouldn't be made for his convenience, to make life simpler for him. He would have to fight like everyone else for what he wanted and needed, even though he was going to a luxurious home in a location he knew nothing about and had never been to before. But it was what he wanted now, total anonymity, while he contemplated how to start his life over and where to begin.

It still felt overwhelming whenever he thought about it. He was going to miss Frances terribly, his little magical elf, who performed miracles for him, like finding him the house where he could hide for the next six months until he felt ready to face the world again. He wasn't ready to yet by any means, and the decision to go to a little town in England felt right to him. Sitting around the house in LA, with nothing to do, too embarrassed to go anywhere and show his face, had been killing him.

As the tensions of the decision eased, and the worries about the paparazzi and the press, Andy relaxed and slept for most of the flight. He had croissants and coffee when he woke up, shortly before they landed, and looked out the window at the British countryside beneath them.

Frances had arranged a car and driver for him, and he hoped to get to the house around seven P.M. if there wasn't too much traffic on the way. The people at the bank had emailed him the alarm code, and the keys had been left under a potted plant near the back door. Since there was no live-in staff, there would be no one to let him in on a Sunday evening. The two women who worked there would arrive at eight the next morning and leave at five. All he knew about them was that the housekeeper was Mrs. MacInnes, and Brigid was the maid. The manager/groundskeeper would check in with him once a week, and the gardeners were from a service hired by the bank. The bankers had already explained that the gardeners weren't planting or maintaining the gardens, they were just keeping it all tidy enough to make the house attractive to potential buyers. The new owners would have to restore the gardens and replant them where necessary. Likewise with minor repairs on the house. Andy didn't know anything else about the house, or the staff. He hoped it didn't look too different from the photographs Frances had shown him on the internet, and that it wasn't a total disaster. The bank had been very minimal with their information, other than dimensions and number of rooms, and when the house had been built, and then later remodeled in its current, slightly ostentatious form. He was still curious about who had owned it and how they had lost it. Clearly, their funds had evaporated if the bank had reclaimed the house.

Andy went through customs without a problem, and the driver found him when he came through immigration. He was holding up a small sign that said "Westfield." He was wearing a uniform and a cap, and had a Mercedes to drive Andy for the rest of the trip. There was heavy traffic on the road, so they got there close to eight. They came on the A259, driving past the town of Winchelsea to the town of Winchelsea Beach on the coast. Andy had slept the entire way. He realized now how exhausted he was from the stress of the past weeks.

He felt like someone had pulled the plug on him. He had only said a few words to the driver, at the airport, and then had fallen into a sound sleep in the back seat.

Once they arrived at the area, all he could see was the quaint little town they drove past and the moon over the water when they got to the beach town. There were no houses near the one he had rented. They stopped at two stone pillars and a tall electric gate. Frances had given the car service the gate code, and the gate opened easily when the driver entered the code into the keypad.

There was a long driveway with a three-story stone house at the end of it, and the lights were on in most of the windows. The housekeeper had come in and turned them on that afternoon, so it would look cheerful when he arrived. Andy looked for the keys in the hiding place the bank had described to Frances, and he found them easily. He could see now that it was a handsome stone house that had probably been built in the 1920s or 1930s, and had been remodeled more recently, as confirmed by the bank. There was a shiny black painted door, with a big brass modern knocker. The door swung open when he unlocked it and he turned off the alarm with the code he'd been given. He told the driver he could leave his bag in the front hall, and thanked him, and he left. Andy was left alone to explore the house.

He was standing in an entrance hall with a black

and white marble floor, which hadn't been in the photographs, but looked stylish, and the living room was a few steps down from there, with a black marble fireplace, and what looked like expensive furniture, in cream-colored fabrics. It was more formal than anything in his own home and would have been a good room to entertain in, which he wouldn't be doing. There was a handsome library, with leather-covered furniture and big comfortable chairs that looked almost new. The art on the walls was modern and most of it was attractive. There was a formal dining room he knew he'd never use, and a big high-tech kitchen, which again suggested that the previous owners had done a lot of entertaining. But the kitchen was a cheerful room with a dining area that opened out into the garden. He opened the door to take a look, but it was too dark to see much, and there was a fussy powder room for guests, with pink wallpaper and a fancy crystal chandelier that looked French.

The staircase to the second floor had an elegant sweep to it. There were four large bedrooms, and a very big master suite with two dressing rooms, and a small sitting room / study, where he could see himself spending quiet evenings, or in the library downstairs, which was more masculine. Everything was in pristine condition, and it gave him the feeling that the owners would return any minute. He checked the closets in the dressing room to make sure they were empty, and they were, every room had its own bathroom, and the master suite had two. It looked almost like a London house, except that it was a little more relaxed, and he decided to explore the top floor the next day. He vaguely remembered Frances telling him that there were old servants' rooms upstairs that were being used as storerooms, and one with some relatively new gym equipment, which he might use if he felt restless or ambitious. He felt almost guilty having such a nice house, just for him, and he would only use part of it. Now that he'd seen it, the rent seemed even more reasonable. He was surprised that the bank hadn't been able to sell it in three years, but it was out of step with the area, which seemed better suited for beach cottages or small country homes. This was too formal, and too decorated for a beach town off the beaten path. He felt lucky to have found it. Six months there suddenly seemed even more appealing with such a comfortable place to stay. He had plenty of room for Wendy and Peter and their children if they came to visit at any point. There was no pool, but they had the sea and the beach in walking distance, which he wanted to see the next day.

He opened the fridge in the kitchen and saw that the housekeeper had left him enough groceries to make breakfast. He helped himself to a bottle of water and walked from room to room again, turning off the lights as he went. He had found an iPad with instructions about what it controlled: the curtains in every room, a stereo system, the alarm, which he didn't bother to turn on, and the lights in every room. The owners had spared no expense modernizing the house, and then had lost it. It seemed like a shame to him. It was a waste of a lovely home that had obviously been someone's main residence and not a beach house for occasional use.

He carried his suitcase upstairs and left it in his dressing room, which had built-ins for a man's wardrobe, and he saw that the large TV in the bedroom was connected to the iPad too. He didn't bother to turn it on, although it might have been nice to hear voices in the house. It was totally silent. There were no city noises or signs of life to break the silence, but this was exactly what he had said he wanted, to get away from everyone and everything and have peace. He smiled as he took off his jacket. "Beware of what you wish for," he said out loud, and then sat down at the desk in the small study, put his laptop on the desk, and sent Frances and Wendy texts saying that he had arrived safely. It was lunchtime in California, and mid-afternoon for Wendy and her family in Greenwich. He added on the text to Frances that the house was terrific, better even than the pictures and just what he had wanted.

She had been waiting to hear from him and texted

back immediately. She was thrilled to read that he liked it. She lived to please him and make his life easier, and had for fifteen years. This might have been the last thing she would ever do for him if she took another job, so it meant a lot to her to know that he was happy. She hoped it had been the right move, although going to England had been an impulsive decision that had worried her at first, but maybe he was right. He needed a positive change in his life, and for now this was it.

He checked the bed, and it was made with clean sheets. He noticed that they were an expensive French brand that he had in his guest rooms in LA. They almost matched the curtains in the bedroom, with blue and red flowers, and he suspected that a decorator had done the home, and not a cheap one. He had complained himself at the price of the sheets. He had told his own decorator that for that amount, he could have bought a small car, and she had responded that his guests couldn't sleep in a car. She had a point.

He unpacked his valise and put everything away, which he liked to do as soon as he arrived, although he didn't usually do it himself. He realized that he was about to discover how other people lived, without the benefit of power and having his every thought and need anticipated, but he liked feeling independent too, and proving to himself that he wasn't actually as spoiled as he knew he was.

After he unpacked, he took a shower and relaxed in the strong jet of a powerful showerhead with numerous settings. Every possible luxury seemed to have been installed in the home. It was easy to see where the money had gone. The owners had spent a fortune remodeling and furnishing the house, with every comfort and high-tech device. It made the transition for him very easy, there was nothing quaint or old-fashioned there, and he could see that he was going to be extremely comfortable during his stay. There had been no shock or bad surprises on his arrival. As always, Frances had done her homework well.

He got into the bed and enjoyed the feel of the fresh, impeccably pressed sheets on his skin, and lay in bed smiling. So far, his sudden decision to leave LA and come to England had been a good one. There had been no disappointment. The house was an excellent surprise, and he was still curious about the owners and how they had lost it. He felt a little bit like a gatecrasher, or a squatter, being there. All the trappings of their previously luxurious life were still there, and he was enjoying it all immensely.

He turned the TV on for a few minutes before he went to sleep, and there was nothing interesting on. It was late, even if early for him on LA time, but it had been a long flight, and he turned off the TV and the lights and drifted off to sleep in his cozy new hideaway. He was going to discover the beach and the town in the morning.

When Andy woke up, he had slept for eight hours. It was a beautiful spring day outside. He put on jeans and a black sweater and boots and went downstairs to the kitchen to make breakfast. He was starving, and was startled to see a serious-looking, austere woman standing in the kitchen in an apron. She had gray hair and didn't smile when she saw him.

"Good morning, sir," she said formally. "I'm Mrs. MacInnes, the housekeeper. May I make you breakfast?"

"Thank you very much," Andy said with a warm smile.

"Would you like tea, sir, or coffee?"

"Coffee would be great, black, no sugar." There was a fancy coffeemaker that looked as though it could make espresso and cappuccino too, but he preferred black coffee in the morning.

"Did you sleep well?" she asked, as she made toast for him, and fried eggs after he asked for them.

"Like a baby. It's an incredibly comfortable house. I'm surprised it hasn't sold for three years. It has every high-tech feature. The owners must have spent a fortune on it."

"They did," she confirmed, with a disapproving look.

"Is the bank asking too much for it?"

"No." She hesitated and then added, "The house has a reputation that doesn't appeal to some people. And it's too fancy for people around here. They want simple beach cottages, not a house like this." He was curious about her comment that the house had a reputation. He wondered if the owners were drug dealers. They certainly had had money at their disposal, for a while anyway. He couldn't conceive of the house as a brothel. It was much too elegantly done. It looked like a very stylish house in London or LA. "It's going to be auctioned off in six months, if it doesn't sell before then," she informed him. "It'll probably go for next to nothing. Are you interested in buying it?" she asked, curious about him too. She knew he was from LA, but nothing more than that. He looked like a decent sort to her. She wondered if he was married, but he had come alone. Maybe he was getting divorced.

"I don't think so," Andy said about buying the house. "I have a house in LA."

"Are you in the movie business, sir?" she asked, as she poured him another cup of coffee. The eggs had been delicious. He hesitated before he answered. He wasn't in any business right now. He hadn't figured out yet how he was going to answer that question in future, to people who didn't know the story. It was a relief to be in a place where they didn't.

"I was" seemed the simplest answer, and she nodded. She wasn't sour, but she was serious, as though she hadn't had an easy life. And with that, a young woman with blond hair in pigtails hurried into the kitchen and gave a start when she saw Andy. She blushed bright red.

"Oh, I'm sorry. I didn't know you were here. I thought you were still sleeping."

"This is Brigid," Mrs. MacInnes introduced her.

"Hello," Andy said with a smile, and the girl smiled back.

"I'll go up to do your room now," she said, and left as quickly as she'd arrived.

"Did you work for the previous owners?" Andy asked Mrs. MacInnes, and she nodded.

"I did." She offered no further information, and seemed closed tight, like an oyster.

"What happened?"

She took a long time to answer the question. "They were a family. They're not anymore."

"Divorce?" She nodded and took his dishes to the sink to rinse them, turned her back and turned on the water. It was obvious she didn't wish to say more, out of loyalty, or British restraint. Whatever the reason, she made it clear that she had nothing more to say about them, and he went back to wondering if they were high-end drug dealers of some kind. There was a story there, he could tell, but she wasn't going to share it.

After breakfast, he asked Mrs. MacInnes the way

to the beach, and which way the village was, and she told him. There was a path at the end of the garden which eventually led to the beach. And the village was just a few miles down the road. He asked if she had the car keys, and she took them out of a drawer.

"Bertie, the groundskeeper, started them both yesterday, and put petrol in them. No one's driven them in three years, but he drives them occasionally to keep them going." Andy took the keys to the Land Rover and put the ones to the station wagon back in the drawer.

He went out to look for the garage. It was behind the house. Both cars were clean and seemed in good order. He decided to visit the village first and have a look around. He had to remind himself to drive on the other side of the road from what he was used to. It was a three-mile drive to the village and he was there in minutes. It was a quaint, funny old town with a high street of a few shops, a bookstore, two banks, a post office, two pubs that weren't open so early, and an antique shop. He walked past them and peered into them. He liked the old-fashioned look of the town. There were people buying groceries at the grocery stores and going into the post office. There was a year-round population, and a summer community. He was neither, or both, a visiting observer, and he liked what he saw. He thought he might try eating at the pubs, since he didn't like cooking for himself.

He wandered around town for half an hour and drove back to the house. And then he went back out on foot and looked for the beach. The path was discreetly hidden by hedges and bushes, but he found it according to Mrs. MacInnes's instructions, and it was beautiful and rugged. There were low cliffs further down the beach and jagged rocks bordering a long beach of coarse sand and small weathered pebbles. It didn't look like the sandy California beaches he was used to, but it was nice to walk along and see the channel, which led to the ocean. There was a breeze and short whitecaps, some sailboats farther out moving at a good speed, and fishing boats in the distance. He walked until he came to the small port. There was a dock, and some sailboats covered and tied up, and the berth where the fishing boats came in at night. It all had a rugged feeling to it. He sat down on the beach for a while, enjoying the scene and feeling his soul come to life again. It felt good just being here and smelling the ocean and salt air. There were two children playing on the little pebbles with their mother. They were collecting rocks and putting them in a bucket. He smiled watching them. There was something healthy and peaceful about the place. He'd been lucky, blind luck. Frances had picked a good place, with a supremely comfortable house. He could see himself there for several months easily and maybe even into the summer.

He sat on the beach for a while and then he walked

back in the direction he had come from, and half-
way back he saw a woman with her long dark hair
flying in the breeze. She had her head down and
was walking toward him. She seemed small and
very slight, and at first he wasn't sure if she was a
young girl or a woman, but she had the determined
walk of an adult. She stopped several times and
looked out to sea as he approached, until finally
he was only a few feet away from her as she turned
and looked straight at him. He could see tears glis-
tening on her face in the sunlight. She didn't try
to hide them, and she looked right through him.
She looked ravaged and he almost wanted to go to
her and ask her if she was all right, but it seemed
like it would have been an intrusion. She walked
past him then. She looked young, with her long
hair flying around her, and what had struck him
was that she looked heartbroken. The vision of her
troubled him all the way back to the house, and
he wondered if he should have said something to
her after all, but the moment had passed and she'd
walked on. She'd been wearing a blue denim skirt
and a purple sweater. She looked like a local.

Andy went to his study when he got back, and
answered a slew of emails from his lawyer, his ac-
counting firm, and his investment advisor. The
business of life and responsibility went on with or
without a job. There were invitations that should be
answered, all to be declined, and pages his attorney
needed him to sign for the severance package. He

realized he would have to print them, sign them, and scan and email them back. He missed Frances more than ever and wondered how he was going to manage with no office help at all for the next six months, if he stayed that long. Even if he didn't, he was going to be working as his own assistant, and the idea didn't appeal to him much. He went to talk to Mrs. MacInnes, but she had left for the day by then, and when he called the local bank that managed the house, they were closed. He decided to call them in the morning. Maybe they could suggest someone to help him for a few hours a day with office work. Some local girl who didn't need a full-time job.

Mrs. MacInnes had bought him some groceries and he made a light meal for himself. He watched a movie on TV that night and went to bed early. He was aware that he was lonely and far from home, but he would have been lonelier in LA, where he had become a pariah overnight. No one would want to know him now. That was how it worked. When you were on top, everyone loved you, and when you fell off the mountaintop, you were no one, instantly. He hadn't wanted to experience that in LA. The tables restaurants wouldn't have for him, the people who suddenly didn't remember him. The salespeople who ignored him, the headwaiters with short memories, the adversaries he'd had who rejoiced in his fall and would gloat, the friends he thought he had who would turn out not to be.

He had seen it all happen to others, and he had spared himself that by coming to England. It would seem cowardly to some people, but most of them wouldn't care. He had flown away, out of range, out of mind, out of memory. He had a feeling his father would have told him to stand his ground and face them. And he would one day. But not now. Not yet. He was happy where he was, and for now, it felt like where he was meant to be. He was still wounded and needed time to heal. And the house in Winchelsea Beach seemed like the perfect place to do it.

Chapter 6

Andy called the local bank when he got up the next morning. He spoke to the person Frances had contacted to wire his deposit and the rent for the house, and asked if she knew anyone who might be interested in some secretarial work a few hours a day, nothing full-time and mostly computer work, responding to correspondence and general emails. The woman at the bank was very pleasant, said she'd ask around and call him back.

He took another walk on the beach then, and had an idea. There was no one he wanted to talk to at the moment, except for one man he knew in London and would like to see again, Dash Hemming. They'd put together one film. Dash was an independent film producer. He was English and a particularly nice guy. He was younger than Andy, in his early forties, but they had enjoyed meeting in LA, and Andy had promised to contact him when he went to England. Dash wasn't part of the studio rat race, which was why he stayed independent. He wanted no part of all that, and said he admired Andy for how sane he had remained after nineteen years of it.

"Cowboy blood in my veins," Andy had said, and they both laughed. "My father was the most unflappable man I've ever met. I have a little of that. You need it in this business."

Andy found Dash Hemming's number in the contacts on his phone and decided to call him on the spur of the moment, and was surprised when Dash answered the office number himself. He was amazed to hear Andy at the other end.

"Now that's a surprise," he said, sounding pleased. "What the hell just went on over there? I couldn't believe what I read. It was a stupid move to sell, and even dumber to lose you. They'll be up to their ears in shit and begging you to come back in six months." A few others had said the same, but not many.

"I doubt that. They'll figure it out without me."

"You had it nailed. I've never seen a big studio operate like that. Smooth as silk. Dumbass corporate jocks, they don't know their asses from a hole in the ground, and they think that anyone can run this business and make movies. The new guy in your seat has no experience."

"I didn't either when I started. You learn."

"Damn few do. You're smarter than all of them

put together. So, what are you doing now? You should be making independent movies. At least you'd have fun doing it." Dash loved what he did, and did it well. Andy respected him too, it was mutual.

"I'm not sure I'd be good at it. That's your talent, not mine. My father always wanted to do one, but he didn't need to. He had the studios at his feet. It makes a difference when you go in as a big star."

"When are you coming to England? It would be great to see you," Dash asked. He was a big burly guy, and looked like a teddy bear with a beard, and he was a terrific producer. Andy admired his work. But making an indie film didn't appeal to him. He liked the big business of the studio and running the show at a much higher level. It was what he did best.

"I'm here, actually," Andy said, feeling a little sheepish. He hadn't told anyone else what he'd done, except Wendy. "I figured LA was going to be unbearable for a while. The press, the paparazzi, the gossip, the bullshit. So I ran. I rented a house here for six months, and I thought I'd float around Europe for a while. I'm becoming a beachcomber," he said wryly.

"You're in London?" Dash sounded stunned.

"No, I'm in Winchelsea Beach. My assistant found a house on the internet, and five days later, I flew here. This is my second day. So far so good."

"How on earth did you settle on that town, of all

places?" Dash laughed at the image of Andy there. He imagined him in a small beach cottage, in a place that was asleep ten months a year.

"It's the only place she found with central heating that wasn't a one-room dollhouse in the Cotswolds."

"Well, for God's sake, come to London, and let's have a drink. Let's have quite a lot of drinks," he said jovially.

"I will," Andy promised, "and you're welcome here anytime. I have guest rooms and the house is surprisingly nice. It's up for sale, and I have it for six months."

"I'll try to come see you. I'm glad you called. And listen, you know things will calm down in LA eventually. It won't stay hot forever. But I'm glad you're here for now. It was a smart move, although I'm not sure that Winchelsea is so smart. You might die of boredom there." Dash laughed again. "At least it's not winter. It's pretty damn bleak there in winter. You've got to come to London. We'll go pub crawling together."

"Sounds good," Andy said, glad he had called him. Dash was a real person, and not part of the Hollywood hype.

"Stay in touch."

"I will, for sure," Andy said.

When he hung up, the woman at the local bank called him and said she had someone in mind for secretarial assistance. She didn't know if it would work out, but she had called the woman, and she seemed interested. The banker had taken the liberty of telling the woman to go to the house at five o'clock to meet him, but said she could cancel it if it wasn't convenient for Andy, or if he preferred to make the appointment himself.

"No, that's perfect," Andy said enthusiastically. The emails had continued to roll in, and he needed assistance. "What's her name?"

The woman hesitated for a second. "Violet Smith," she said smoothly. "She hasn't worked for a while, but she's bright and capable. I hope it works out," she said briskly, and they hung up.

Andy was pleased. It had been a good morning. He had enjoyed talking to Dash Hemming, and he had an assistant on the way. He had a dozen emails he needed to print out, sign, and scan back. And he read through his emails again that afternoon, and there were more. Frances would have handled them in minutes, but on his own, he felt swamped.

He explored the third floor that afternoon, and all the old servants' rooms were filled with boxes and furniture. There was one whole room of children's furniture and toys. They hadn't even taken their children's toys with them. For a minute, Andy felt sorry for the owners. They had left everything. But there were no rooms up there he wanted to use anyway, so he didn't mind. He saw the gym equipment but didn't want to use it yet. And there was no one to carry it downstairs for him.

He read through a big email from his financial advisor, with his suggestions of what to do with the severance money, and by the time he finished, it was a few minutes before five. Violet Smith arrived promptly. Mrs. MacInnes had just left and Andy opened the door to her himself. He was surprised by how attractive she was, and there was something vaguely familiar about her, he didn't know why. She had dark hair pulled tightly back. She had big violet-colored eyes, a deep purplish blue, and creamy milk-white English skin. As he looked at her, he thought of Snow White in the fairy tale. She was wearing a caramel-colored twin sweater set, leather pants the same color, and high heels. Simply but elegantly dressed for the interview, she looked more like London than Winchelsea Beach. She followed him in and seemed stiff and uncomfortable. He escorted her into the library and invited her to sit down. He saw her looking around and he explained that he had just arrived and was renting the house for six months. And as he spoke to her, he realized she was the woman he had seen crying on the beach and continued talking to her without acknowledging that he'd seen her before. And she showed no sign of remembering him.

"I just got here from LA." He described the emails he had received and the help he needed from her. "It's not a very exciting job, I'm afraid. It's mostly faxes and emails, and scanning, maybe a few phone calls to LA. It's not a full day's work.

I was thinking that maybe you could come every morning, say till lunchtime. Would that be enough for you?" he asked, and she nodded. She seemed very shy, and he guessed her to be in her early or mid-thirties. Then she surprised him by saying she was thirty-eight. She said it was on her CV, which he hadn't read yet. She had handed it to him when she walked in. It was information she didn't have to give him but she had anyway. She hadn't worked in a long time, and things had changed.

"Are you in a job now?" he asked her. "Or are you working part-time somewhere else?" She was well dressed and didn't look like she needed to work. She was well-spoken, and from what he could tell, sounded like she was from an educated upper-class British background.

"No, I'm not in a job. Actually, I haven't worked in eleven years. I was a journalist in London for The **Sunday Times.** I got married and moved here, and I haven't worked since then. I've been doing odd jobs and part-time for the past several months. I need to get back in the work force. I should probably go back to London, but eleven years is a long time to be out of work. I'm not really up-to-date anymore, except for something like this. My computer skills are pretty basic, but I can certainly scan and email." She smiled at him, and he saw how pretty she was when she did. She was a serious-looking woman, and she hadn't smiled until then.

He wondered if she was married, but couldn't

ask. He preferred single assistants, like Frances. Their personal lives didn't interfere, and Violet was a reasonable age. She was not some wild twenty-two-year-old, out dancing every night and hungover the next day.

She volunteered the information on her own. "I'm no longer married and I don't have children." He noticed that she looked sad when she said it, but he didn't comment.

"Well, what do you think, Violet? It's not an exciting job, but I definitely need help. Would it suit you?" She was obviously intelligent and over-qualified for the job, but that was a plus for him, if it didn't bother her. He guessed at what seemed like a fair rate to him, and her eyes widened in surprise when he said it.

"I hope I'll be worth that," she said softly, "and yes, the job would suit me very well. When would you like me to start?"

"Is tomorrow too soon?"

She smiled at his answer. "That's fine with me. I've been filling in at the bookshop, but they can manage very well without me. I told them I was coming for an interview, and I can still help them on weekends." Andy had a feeling that she needed the money, although she didn't look it. She looked very well put together, and her clothes looked expensive. She had a well-brought-up look to her.

"You can dress casually for work. We won't be

seeing anyone. It's just the housekeeper and her helper here, and myself."

"Are jeans okay sometimes?" she asked cautiously. "Not every day."

"Fine. Any other questions?" She said she had none, and five minutes later, she left, and he saw that she had come on a bicycle. She seemed like a very nice woman, and none of the work he had for her was complicated. He felt sure she was more than capable of it.

She arrived promptly at nine the next morning, and Andy was waiting for her in the study with a list of the emails he needed to have printed. There were a lot of them.

She had worn a navy blue twin set and jeans, with a string of pearls and running shoes, and got right to work, checking his list. She was working in the library on the main floor. He had offered her tea or coffee, which she declined.

"We need a printer, I'm afraid," he told her, "and there's one on the inventory, but I can't find it, and the housekeeper didn't know where it is either. There are half a dozen servants' rooms upstairs jammed full of boxes and the owners' belongings. I hope it's not up there. It will take us hours to find it."

"I doubt it would be, Mr. Westfield," she said

primly. "I think I know where it might be." She stood up from the desk, walked to the far wall, took out a section of four books, reached in and pressed a button, and a whole section of what looked like bookshelves with leather-bound books on them came forward and revealed a large storage space behind it. The printer and a computer were there. She took both out, and some other supplies and paper she needed to print. Andy stared at her in amazement.

"How did you know that was there?" he asked her.

"A lot of these old houses have secret passages and false walls," she said quietly, "and even when a new owner remodels, they usually preserve things like that. It was just a guess," she said modestly. Andy was still stunned.

"That's incredible. Do you think there's a secret passage here too?"

"I don't, but we can always look. They're hard to find and harder to maintain, and I always think they're dangerous with children in the house. So if they did have one, they might have sealed it up." She clearly knew what she was talking about, as Andy realized that there was more to Violet Smith than one guessed initially. She had a Lois Lane quality, the young woman in **Superman** who had hidden superpowers. She set up the printer without making a fuss, and twenty minutes later she had all his emails printed and ready to sign. And as soon as he did, she scanned and emailed them to the people who had sent them and were waiting for his signature on a variety of documents, most of them financial.

She printed out several more that had come in after that. Andy was in the kitchen getting something cold to drink when Violet came in for a cup of tea and Mrs. MacInnes's face brightened and she smiled warmly. Andy hadn't seen the housekeeper smile yet until then. She was pleasant, polite, but a very dour woman. But with Violet she looked genuinely delighted to see her.

"How are you?" she asked her, and Violet responded quietly.

"I'm fine." She smiled, gently touched the housekeeper's shoulder, and went back to the study to finish her work. She had been very professional with Andy all morning, but clearly the two women knew each other personally. It was a very small town, so not surprising that they'd met, or were friends.

Everything was finished at one o'clock. Violet's desk was impeccably neat, and she had done everything Andy needed her to do. He couldn't resist asking her as she got ready to leave, "Have you worked here before?"

"No," she said quietly. "I know Mrs. MacInnes from town. We shop at the same market, and she comes into the bookshop quite a lot. We have a lending library there too." The explanation sounded reasonable to him. After Violet left, he made himself a sandwich in the kitchen and chatted with Mrs. MacInnes when she walked in.

"I noticed that you and Violet know each other," he said, fishing a little. He was still curious about Violet, and what she was doing in Winchelsea Beach. It seemed like a dead end for her. "She said you met at the bookshop. She's a lovely woman and very efficient."

"She's a wonderful person. It's a shame she has to work," Mrs. MacInnes said with feeling, obviously sympathetic. "At least she'll be treated well here." She had already decided that Andy seemed like a kind man. "She's fallen on hard times," she volunteered, which made sense to him, given the way Violet spoke and the clothes she wore.

"I'm surprised she's not working in London," Andy said.

"She probably can't afford to move. London's expensive. She can live more cheaply here, and the realtor hadn't told them and maybe didn't know."

"She'd make more money there," Andy said. It was a catch-22, and it sounded as though Violet was trapped where she was, which was good luck for him. He still couldn't get over her guesswork with the bookcase. That was quite a trick. He would never have known the false wall was there, and the realtor hadn't told them and maybe didn't know.

As promised, Violet came to do his office work for him, five half days a week, and everything he needed got done. She kept to herself and spoke very little and was willing to do whatever project he asked of her. She was resourceful when she needed to be, creative, intelligent, and vastly overqualified as he had guessed, but she didn't feel demeaned by the job. She thanked him regularly for the opportunity. She was respectful, pleasant, and discreet, and never spoke of herself. In some ways she reminded him of Frances in the beginning, when she was still young and very shy. He had come to realize that Violet wasn't so much shy as reserved. She had strong boundaries that she enforced, and although Andy was aware that she knew Mrs. MacInnes, she didn't visit in the kitchen and try to hang out with her. She stayed in the library, which she used as an office. Maybe because she was British, she was even more formal and old-school than Andy. He had encouraged her after the first day to call him by his first name, which she did, but she was always respectful.

He had so much financial work the second week that she worked all day Friday, until after six o'clock, and she didn't complain about having to stay late when they finished at almost seven o'clock. She was in a hurry when she left. She was having dinner with a friend, and pedaled off on her bicycle with a wave at Andy, and wished him a good weekend. He couldn't help wondering if she had a boyfriend, she was such a good-looking woman. He hated to think of women like Violet and Frances being alone, and there were so many of them. They didn't get out in the world to meet someone, were either justifiably afraid of the internet or had had bad experiences with it, and many had few opportunities in their jobs to meet men. In Violet's case, none at all. Andy had no visitors to his office in Winchelsea Beach, and he had had very few suitable single male visitors, other than major movie stars, for Frances in LA. He hoped that Frances would meet a good guy in her new job.

After Violet left his house on Friday night, Andy poured himself a scotch from the bar in the library. He hadn't had a drink since the previous weekend, but he was feeling relaxed and had nothing to do. He still hadn't tried eating at the local pubs. He didn't like dining out alone and was living mostly on takeaway food. He noticed a folder on Violet's desk that didn't look familiar, and wondered if she had started a new filing system of her own. He opened the file and was surprised to see what looked like a manuscript for a book. He flipped through the pages and saw that there were three chapters, and he saw Violet's name carefully written on the inside cover. Feeling like a thief, he sat down on the couch with it, and read it straight through with a second scotch. It was beautifully written, a gripping story of a woman held in the thrall of a dangerous narcissist with criminal intentions who was blackmailing her, holds her hostage, and plans to kill her. Andy was frustrated when the last chapter ended, and he wanted to read more. There were no further chapters in the folder. It was a fantastic story, and would make an excellent book, and even better movie. He put it back on the desk, thinking of Violet, a woman of carefully hidden talents. She had mentioned nothing about her writing skills in the interview. He couldn't wait to ask her about it on Monday, although he would have to admit that he had read it without her permission. She was a very talented writer, and he couldn't wait to see her and ask her about it, and if she had written more yet.

She was an intriguing woman, and something about her quiet demeanor suggested to him that she had secrets. And the sadness he had glimpsed on the beach haunted him.

His own life was an open book to her now, or very nearly. The correspondence she had read and scanned from his lawyer talked about his severance agreement from Global Studios, as did the emails from his investment advisor. If she read between the lines, she would know that he had been fired from somewhere. It didn't take much to piece the story together, and she was a bright woman. She had signed a standard confidentiality form when she came to work for him, and he wondered how much she had figured out. She hadn't said anything to him, or asked. She was very discreet and polite.

*   *   *

As Andy had guessed, Violet was intrigued by his emails. She hadn't figured out all of it, but it was clear that he had been fired, and the name Global Studios was in some of the correspondence. The payments had come from two different corporations, both AMCO, which she was familiar with, and FAQTS, which she had never heard of. The payments were for an astronomical amount of money, although she had seen amounts like it before, and bigger. She was more worldly than she appeared. She had seen things that Andy could never have dreamed of. But she was sure that Andy was an honest man. In the two weeks she'd been there, he never talked about his job, and she wasn't sure if he was retired or still working, and if he might be working remotely from England. He seemed to be taking time off from his job, whatever it was, and even in the informal setting of the house he had rented, she could sense how important he was in the world from the way people addressed him in their emails.

Feeling guilty for doing so, she looked him up on the internet that weekend, and saw all the recent articles about his being fired in the sale of Global Studios. She was shocked to read that he had been head of the studio for nineteen years and had been fired summarily. And then she realized what he was doing in England. He was licking his wounds, and probably figuring out what to do next. She felt sorry for him when she had read it all. What they had done to him sounded cruel and unfair to her. Violet knew about cruel and had been there herself. But she hated to see it happen to someone else, and he seemed like a kind, honorable man. She could only imagine how much he must be hurting now, particularly to have come so far from his home, to live in a strange house, in a country not his own.

She thought about him all weekend, and had new compassion for him. She didn't want to let him know that she knew now, but she liked him even better, knowing what he'd been through only a month before. She knew he must still be reverberating from the shock of being fired. She wanted to console him, but dignity and discretion demanded that she not even let on that she knew. They were strangers to each other and she was only his employee. She couldn't say anything, all she could do was live up to his faith in her. She was grateful that he had asked her nothing personal about herself since the interview. She had wounds of her own that she had no desire to share, with him or anyone else.

Chapter 7

Andy was eager for Violet to arrive while he finished his breakfast and coffee on Monday morning. He had read Violet's chapters again the night before, and they read even better the second time than the first. Her story was fantastic, and so was the pace. Her writing was smooth and beautiful, the story was gripping, the characters strong. He wanted to know about the story and how much of it she had written, if there was more, or was she just starting? She was a talented writer.

Violet came to say hello to him in the kitchen when she got to work. He thought she looked relaxed and in good spirits, and she and Mrs. MacInnes smiled at each other. Andy got up as soon as he saw her, walked to the study with her, and asked her to sit down. She looked suddenly frightened. He was so serious that she was afraid he was going to fire her.

"Did I do something wrong?" she asked, and looked on the verge of tears.

"No, far from it. I want to ask you about this." He turned and took the folder off the table and held it so she could see it, and she went pale.

"I'm sorry, Andy. I shouldn't have. It's some papers of mine. I brought it to work to use your copy machine. The one in town is always broken. I should have asked you before copying my own papers without your permission."

"You can make a hundred copies of what's in this folder, as long as you give me one of them," he said. "Violet, these are among the best opening chapters I've ever read, and the others were by famous professionals. This is brilliant. I apologize to you for reading it. You left the file on the desk. I opened it on Friday night, and I saw what was in it. I was curious and read it. So, I apologize to you. What are you doing with it? Are you writing a book? I read it again last night and I couldn't put it down. I liked it even better the second time." Her dark violet eyes looked huge in her face.

"I'm trying to write a book. I've always wanted to, but I didn't have time, or the courage. I've only been working on this for a few months. And yes, there's more. I've almost finished it. I'm working on the last chapter now. But the rest is all handwritten. I haven't typed it up yet. I've only typed the first three chapters, which is why I brought them in to copy on Friday."

"Then I have a proposition to make you. I will pay you for full days, till five every day, and when you finish my work at one every day, you can spend the rest of the day typing your manuscript. I want you to finish this soon. You are sitting on an absolutely spectacular piece of work. And I have a question to ask you. Do you want to try to have this published as a book, or would you like to turn it into a screenplay? You could publish the book afterward, if you wanted to, or the reverse, and have a movie follow the book. It's incredibly cinematic, and I think you should do it first as a screenplay. I can find someone to work with you if you want, or even help you do it." Andy paused then, and continued to look at her. "You've been scanning my legal and financial correspondence for two weeks. I'm sure you've figured out that I was the head of Global Studios for nineteen years. I got fired a month ago when the studio was sold. They said I was protected in the deal, but I wasn't. They signed the deal on Friday night and fired me at nine o'clock on Monday morning. So, to put it bluntly, I'm out of a job and unemployed. I may even stay that way. Studio head positions don't come along very often.

"I was a screenwriter for sixteen years before I got hired to run the studio. I know screenwriting in my sleep, and I've never written anything as strong as you just did. But I can show you how to do it as a screenplay, if you want to do it yourself, and use my connections to set you up with a producer who would help put a deal together for you. You can still publish it as a book, before or after. My son-in-law is a book publisher and I'd be happy to introduce you to him too. Violet, this is big league stuff, and I may have been fired a month ago, but I have all the connections you need to get this project going. I'd like you to use them, if you're willing." Suddenly he laughed as he looked as her. "Hell, maybe I'll be an agent in my next life. And if so, I want to be yours. But seriously, I'd like to help you with this. You have an award-winning piece of work here."

"You would do all that for me? Why?" Violet asked him, with tears in her eyes.

"Because you have an incredible talent, and you're a good person. And you deserve it," he said simply. "Everyone deserves a break sometime, especially with a talent like yours. You have a gold mine here, Violet. Would you let me make some calls for you, to see who might be interested, and who you could send the manuscript to, after you type it up?"

"Of course," she said, breathless over everything he had told her and what he was willing to do for her. It was like the hand of destiny that Andy had rented the house and needed an assistant and the bank had called her.

"May I read the handwritten material you have now, before you type it, so I don't have to wait?" He was eager to see the rest of the story.

"I'll bring it tomorrow morning, or I can go home for it at lunchtime when I finish your work today. I'll bring it for you, and then I'll start typing the rest of what I have. You probably read faster than I type," Violet said, smiling. She felt as though a miracle had happened. "And if you're serious, I think I'd like to do a movie first. They can publish the book later."

"I agree," Andy said, feeling the same way she did about it. The hand of destiny had touched them both. He needed something to occupy his time, and he had the connections she needed. And she had no idea where to go or who to talk to about what she'd written. He could open important doors for her. He knew them all. Big filmmakers, small ones, the studios that were favorable to new writers and unknown talent, the directors, producers, and stars who were constantly looking for scripts. Violet was an extremely talented writer, and her manuscript deserved to see the light of day. She had written big league material in this fusty old beach town in England. Andy was blown away and determined to help her.

He had very little work for her that day, and she went home as promised at lunchtime and brought back what she'd written, longhand. It was all there except for the last chapter, which she hadn't completed yet. She wanted to do that first.

"What happens in the end?" he asked her.

"He tries to kill her and fails. She has the opportunity to kill him and doesn't. The gun is in her hands, she escapes, the police come, there's a gunfight, she's wounded, but she survives, and they arrest him. He goes to prison."

"A satisfying ending. Is there a love interest?"

Violet shook her head. "No, but there could be. All she does is try to survive and not let him kill her, once she knows what he's done. I could add a love interest," she said, thinking about it.

"You can add that later if you want to. You have all the strong points in the book."

"I feel like I should be paying you, not you paying me to type my own book." She smiled at him.

"I'll bill the producer for it," he teased her. Suddenly they were friends. They had a project that would save them both if they could find a producer and a screenwriter. The producer would do the rest, line up the director, the financing, and the actors. He already had some thoughts about who to call.

Violet looked at Andy gratefully as they sat in the library together.

"I think what they did to you was incredibly unfair, and how they did it," she said softly.

"It was ugly," he admitted, "but it's the nature of the industry. I came in on the heels of the previous CEO when AMCO bought the studio nineteen years ago. Now it's someone else's turn. I was the youngest studio head in the business. Now I'm old and I'm out. They flip it on a dime. The new owner's son wanted my job, and he got it. They paid a small fortune for it. And who knows, maybe he'll be good at it."

"And what will you do?" she asked, worried about him. He had just offered to do so much for her, he had touched her deeply. No one had ever done anything for her before. She had been struggling alone for a long time. She no longer had a family to turn to. Her mother had died of cancer when she was in college, and her father of a heart attack a year later, brokenhearted after his wife's death.

"I have no idea," Andy said about his future. "That's why I'm here. To figure it out. But for now, we're going to try to get you off and running with your story. I'm going to make some calls tonight," he promised. Violet could already sense that he was a man of his word, and she knew he would do what he said. And even if he changed his mind and didn't do it, she would be no worse off than she'd been before. She was used to having people disappoint her and hurt her. Nothing surprised her anymore. That was what Andy saw in her eyes. He could see it in the way she looked at him. She had been wounded. She didn't say it, but he knew. "Trust me, Violet. Something wonderful is going to happen. It may take time. Hollywood moves slowly sometimes, but they're hungry for what you've got," he said, pointing to the folder she'd brought him with the rest of her manuscript. He couldn't wait to read it.

She stopped typing at five o'clock, and he looked at her after Mrs. MacInnes left. "Do you want to stay for something to eat? I don't know what's in the fridge. Probably half a lemon and a banger sandwich," he said, and she laughed.

"Why don't we go to the chippy in town? Do you like fish-and-chips?"

"I love it." They sat and talked for a while longer about the development of her story and the last chapter she hadn't finished yet, and at six o'clock, he put her bike in the Land Rover and drove her into town to the chippy at the end of the high street. It was exciting to be part of a project that wasn't even born yet, with someone as new and fresh and talented as she was.

"Do you have family here, Violet?" he asked her. She seemed too sophisticated for this tiny village.

"No, I don't have family anymore. My parents both died when I was in college. They weren't very old. My mother died of breast cancer, and my father had a heart attack a year later and died too. I think he couldn't live without her. They had a wonderful marriage."

"So did mine," Andy said nostalgically. "Where did you go to college?" It was on her CV, but he'd forgotten.

"I went to the University of Westminster and

majored in journalism, and got my graduate degree in journalism from the London School of Economics. I grew up in London. And after LSE, I got the job at **The Sunday Times,** and not long after, I got married and moved here." She made it sound very simple and had an excellent education.

"And you don't want to go back to London?"

"I might one day, but I can't afford to right now. Life is much cheaper in a village like this." She seemed resigned to her fate and didn't complain about it. But it was obvious to him that she didn't belong there. She had been brought up and educated for a much bigger life.

"You'll be able to move back after this," Andy said confidently. "What have you been living on?" It was an impertinent question, but he felt protective of her, and she could sense it. The loss of her parents had touched him. And he could see how brave she was.

"Odd jobs. The bookshop. You, now. I take care of a few people's summer cottages for them. They don't come here in the winter, so I check on things, and have leaks repaired, and burst pipes. I get by." Listening to Violet made him realize again how fortunate he was, how blessed he had been all his life, with parents who had provided for him and protected him, good jobs as a screenwriter, and then an extraordinary opportunity as a studio head for almost twenty years. He had never been in danger as she was, living hand to mouth, with no family and no one to protect her or be a safety net for her.

"Do you have children?" she asked him, as they ate their shared dinner out of little cardboard boxes.

"One. A daughter. She's happily married with two very sweet children and lives in Connecticut. She and her husband are both in publishing. She's close to your age. She's thirty-two." Andy felt paternal toward Violet now. She was becoming his protégée.

"Thank you for the compliment," Violet said, and looked worldly-wise for a minute. "I'm thirty-eight." He'd seen it on her resumé and forgotten her exact age.

He smiled at her. "I was your age when I became studio head at Global. And now I'm fifty-seven, and I've felt like I'm a hundred for the past month."

"Sometimes I feel that way too," she said, and looked wistful. "Loss is a hard thing to adjust to, but you get used to it," she said, as though she'd been there.

"It's a job. I'll get over it," Andy said, trying not to sound weak to her. He didn't feel right complaining to her. Her life was a great deal harder than his.

"It's still a lot to lose. There must be a lot that goes with those jobs," she said, and he laughed.

"Yeah, a plane, a title, a fancy car, a big office, and everyone kissing your ass. I got very spoiled in nineteen years. This has been humbling. Maybe I deserved it, and it's good for me. You get to feeling very important. No one is ever that important."

"Maybe you'll find something you like better," Violet said.

"It's hard for me to imagine right now, but maybe you're right. I don't know what that would be. I loved my job every day, who wouldn't?" He sounded sad, like a little boy who had lost his favorite toy.

"What did your parents do?" she asked, curious about him, just as he was about her, and he smiled at the question.

"They were movie stars," Andy said simply. "I'm a Hollywood brat. They were way before your time, and a big deal in the States. My father was in Westerns, John Westfield, and my mother was a glamour queen, Eva Lundquist. She was Swedish."

"Oh my God, my father was addicted to your father's movies. He made me watch them all. He said they were the greatest movies of all time, and he had a huge crush on your mother. I've seen some of her movies too. My father was a banker, he was president of a bank, and my mother was a kindergarten teacher and loved it. Pretty normal stuff. I had a very traditional British upbringing and a happy childhood. We didn't have a lot of money, but we were comfortable. I was an only child, and neither of my parents had living relatives. It was just the three of us and we were very close, which made it that much worse when they died. I was totally alone. Your childhood must have been incredibly exciting. Did you have movie stars come to your house all the time?" Violet looked fascinated by what he'd shared with her. It sounded very exotic compared to her early life.

"My parents' movie star friends dropped by just about every day. I thought they were regular people, until I grew up and realized how lucky I was. My parents were good people. That was the best part. They've been gone for a long time. I still miss them." She nodded, as though she understood what that was like, but didn't comment.

When they finished their fish-and-chips, Andy dropped Violet off at her place with her bike. She lived in the tiny village at Winchelsea Beach, not at the inland town, which was Winchelsea. She lived in a little one-room cottage that looked shabby and slightly battered. One of the shutters had fallen off and was on the ground. The house was at the end of the village.

Then he drove home, thinking about her. Something told him that she was a brave woman, and she was certainly a talented one. He was happy he'd met her and that she'd come to work for him.

When Andy got home, he settled into a chair in the library and read the rest of Violet's manuscript. It was every bit as good as the first three chapters, and maintained the tension throughout until the

very end of what she'd given him. He could hardly
wait until the last chapter she was working on. He
had enjoyed dinner with her. He hoped that if she
had some success with her book or movie, she'd
get back to London. She didn't belong in this tiny
place off the beaten track. He thought she deserved
a husband and children, not the loneliness of a
beach town in winter, living from hand to mouth,
relying on tourists like him and the summer renters. She needed a better life than that. He felt fa-
therly toward her.

When Andy got home that night, he placed a
call to Dirk Howard, a producer/director he knew
who was famous for using young talent, and often
bought book properties from unknown writers. He
was young and brash himself, but talented and successful. It was Andy's first call back into Hollywood,
but he wanted to do it for Violet. Howard took the
call immediately. Andy hadn't lost his touch yet. It
was slightly reassuring.

"To what do I owe the honor?" Dirk said as he
came on the line. He was cocky and full of himself. "What are you up to now?" he asked Andy, as
though he had the upper hand. He had no grace at
all, but some very good films to his credit.

"Enjoying myself for a change," Andy said calmly,
in his best imitation of his father, to give him
patience.

"I hear you're living in London."

"Close enough." He wondered who had talked. Maybe a member of his house staff. No one else knew, and Frances would never talk. "I'll get to the point. I read a manuscript I'm impressed with. The woman who wrote it is going to need a screen-writer, and a producer, to turn it into a screenplay. How do you usually package that with someone brand-new with a ton of talent? It's one of the best manuscripts I've read."

"Are you playing agent now?" Dirk asked.

"No, more like godfather. I want to open some doors for her. She'll take off like a rocket after that."

"New girlfriend?" Dirk asked with a sneer in his voice. "You have time to play now. How old is she? Twenty-two, twenty-five? I saw Alana the other day with the new head of Global, by the way. Rumor has it she's working on breaking up his marriage." Dirk was so sleazy he made Andy's skin crawl, but he ignored the rude comments. He hadn't called him as a friend, but as a connection for Violet.

"No, not a girlfriend, just a very talented writer."

"Well, if you're serious about it. I'll tell you what I do. You can do it with writers, they're insecure, it's harder with on-screen talent, and they all have agents. Does she?" Dirk asked.

"No," Andy said bluntly.

"Good. Better yet. First I tell them that what they've written is complete shit and I couldn't give it away if I tried, then I make them an outrageously low offer. A thousand, two, at most five. They cave because most of them are starving and don't have agents yet. I buy it for less than I pay for a leather jacket, and then I own the rights, and I make a fortune on the front and back end if the picture is a hit. You have to pick them right. Whatever you do, don't pay a bunch of money for it, or you'll lose money on the deal. It works like a charm every time."

Andy felt sick as he listened to him, if that was what they were doing to young writers in Hollywood these days.

"Listen, if you think the material is that good, send it to me. If I like it, I'll split it with you, and we'll both make a killing." Dirk had made several killings and now Andy knew how.

"Thanks, Dirk. I'll take another look and get back to you." Andy didn't want to tell Dirk what an utter piece of garbage he thought he was, exploiting new talent to his own benefit. It was why some people in Hollywood hated producers, the sleazy ones. Andy hated the thought of Violet falling into hands like Dirk's. He was filth, without honor or morality, Andy knew now.

"Anytime, Andy. Hell, you never know, we could produce a movie together sometime. With your connections, if you go into production, you could clean up." Andy wasn't about to ruin his reputation with the likes of Dirk Howard. He had thought he was just a jerk, he hadn't realized how profoundly dishonest he was too. There were some great producers in Hollywood with integrity. Dirk Howard wasn't one of them.

"Thanks, Dirk."

"It was great talking to you, good luck!" Dirk said. Andy hung up and stared into space for a minute. He'd been a fool to call Dirk Howard. He was going to call Dash Hemming in the morning and should have called him in the first place. Dash was an honest man, and Andy trusted his judgment. Dash had made some very powerful movies. They were all independent, so he wasn't beholden to anyone, and wasn't under the thumb of a studio, which was how Dash wanted it. If an independent movie was a big box office success, there was real money in it. It was a very different game from a big blockbuster made with a studio. You didn't have the same protections and guarantees. The quality of the production could suffer if a producer wasn't careful. But Andy wasn't worried about quality or reliability if Dash took the project on. He would play it straight with Andy. Andy had deep respect for Dash, and none for Dirk Howard after talking to him.

Andy went to bed that night determined to call Dash in the morning. He would know what to do with Violet's manuscript and if it was viable for one of his movies. Andy wanted to deliver good news to her. She deserved some good luck. Someone did. His had run out, but he hoped that hers was just beginning. And he could sense that underneath her good manners, British reserve, and quiet dignity, she desperately needed it.

Chapter 8

A ndy called Dash as soon as he was dressed the
next morning. He didn't want to call too early
and wake him. He waited politely until nine o'clock,
and called him on his cell. Dash's schedule was always erratic.

"How's life in Winchelsea Beach? Ready to give
up your beach life and come to London? What do
you wear on the beach there? A ski parka?" Dash
loved to tease Andy.

"We've had very fine weather."

"You lie. This is my country. We don't have fine
weather."

"You should move to Miami." Andy dished it
back to him.

"Can I lure you to London to get shamefully
drunk in the pubs with me?"

"As a matter of fact, yes, for the first part. I'm not

sure about the shamefully drunk. I did more than my share of that before I got here."

"I don't blame you," Dash said. "I'd have done a lot worse than that. You're a hero, man, and you're still standing."

"That's debatable. I'd like to have dinner with you. I have a manuscript in my pocket, by an unknown. She's incredibly talented. It's a killer manuscript. I think it should be a film first. She can follow it up with a book later, if the movie is a success. She wrote it as a book."

"So, we'd need a screenwriter," Dash said thoughtfully. "It takes time to find the right one. And they're usually booked up for months, and slow as hell. She couldn't write the script?"

"She's never done it. I think you'd be better off with a pro on that."

"Yeah, me too. So are you thinking of making a little indie film now?" Dash teased him again.

"No, I'm hoping you are. Making indie movies isn't my gig, it's yours," Andy reminded him.

"I'll make a convert of you yet. It's the way to go now. No studio bullshit."

"Maybe. But it's damn hard to put an independent movie together and get the same quality. You're one of the few who does it right. And you do it best."

"Flattery will get you whatever you want. What kind of shape is it in?"

"I think she's got five or six chapters typed. The

rest is all longhand, she still has to type it. She's writing the last chapter now."

"I'll read whatever you've got," Dash said willingly. A studio wouldn't have done that. It had to be clean, digital, finished, and perfectly typed. "I'll read it on cocktail napkins or newspaper, which is how I see most first drafts."

"When can I come to see you?" Andy asked him, and Dash was impressed that Andy was so committed to the property. That told him a lot. Andy Westfield was no fool about movies. His judgment was sound, and his instincts legendary.

"Does tomorrow night work for you?" Dash asked him.

"Perfect."

"What's your part in this?" Dash inquired, curious.

"I just want to make the introduction. After that, if you like what she's got, it's up to you and her. I have no stake in this. I believe in what I'm bringing you. You're the indie guy, I'm not."

"I'd like to change your mind on that. I would love to work with you. It would be an education for me." Dash was a huge fan of Andy's.

"Don't overestimate me. And don't forget, I'm the guy who just got kicked out on my ass."

"They were fools. Corporate assholes. You'll be back on top again, and they'll be sorry."

"Don't be so sure." Dash hated to hear Andy so down, and so unsure of himself. His ego had taken a nuclear hit. It was the nature of the business, especially in the big studios that were owned by corporations and conglomerates now, with the shots being called by people who knew nothing about the business. Andy had movies in his DNA. "Where should I meet you?" Andy asked him.

"The Shed," Dash suggested. "It's near my place. You can carry me home if I get too drunk. Where will you stay, by the way?"

"I always stay at Claridge's."

"Very posh. I'm glad to hear you're not broke. At least they paid you off decently, or I hope they did." Andy had been successful for so long that Dash doubted he was dependent on his job for his lifestyle by now.

"They did," Andy confirmed. It wasn't enough to soothe his ruffled feathers or his broken heart, at least not yet, but it was something. His investment advisor was happy with the influx of a large amount of money, which never hurt.

"See you tomorrow at eight," Dash said. "And Andy, thank you for bringing it to me first." Andy felt mildly guilty about his call to Dirk Howard, but no harm had been done. He was glad he had called Dash.

They hung up, and Andy went straight to the library to find Violet. She was copying what she had written at home the night before. She had stayed up late to do it.

"We've got work to do," he said in his best studio head tone. She wasn't used to that yet so she was startled. "First, I need you to call Claridge's in London, and get me a decent room for tomorrow night. They know which suites I like. And I want them to send me a car and driver at whatever time it needs to be to have me at the hotel at six o'clock." He wanted time to shower and change when he arrived. Dash Hemming always looked like an unmade bed, but Andy Westfield didn't. He was unemployed but he was not going to look a mess, although he was sure the restaurant Dash had picked would be casual.

"Then after you call the hotel, I want you to sit in a chair and type as much as you can of the manuscript, right up until I leave for London tomorrow. I want a copy of it to give a producer I'm seeing in London. And whatever isn't typed, give me a copy of your handwritten material. He's not picky. He'll read it in any form, he said so." Her deep violet eyes were wide as she looked at Andy.

"You're seeing a producer? For me?"

"I am." He smiled at her. She looked terrified. "One of the best. He's an independent filmmaker, which might be the way to go for your first movie. Let's see what he says. I trust him implicitly. I spoke to him this morning. He knows I wouldn't come to him with anything that isn't great. I'm having dinner with him tomorrow night. Now please call Claridge's and start typing."

"I wrote the last chapter last night." Violet looked worried. "Will you look at it and tell me what you think?" Andy had suddenly become her counselor and mentor, and she trusted him. She handed him the pages she'd written the night before, and he took them upstairs to the study off his bedroom to read quietly without distraction. He was back forty-five minutes later, and she was typing furiously. Andy was smiling as he handed it back to her.

"It's perfect. Don't change a word. Perfect ending. How's the typing going? Do you want a cup of tea?"

Violet nodded, amazed by what he was doing for her. "Claridge's said that you'll have one of your usual suites, and the car will be here at three, in case there's heavy traffic."

"Excellent, thank you." He was back five minutes later, set the tea down beside her, and left her alone to work.

She stayed up most of that night to do it, and she had typed all but the last two chapters by the time he left for London the next day. The manuscript was in pretty decent shape. She handed him the copy of the whole thing in a manila envelope, and he slipped it into his briefcase. He smiled at her before he left.

"Now get some sleep and forget about it. It's in my hands and Dash Hemming's. I'll leave it with him. You can trust him."

"I trust you," she said in a hoarse voice. She looked as tired and anxious as she was. "I didn't think anyone would see it this soon. Maybe it's not ready. I should have gone through it again to polish it."

"It's ready. Go home and get some sleep. I won't have any news for you when I get back. He won't have time to read it before I leave, so don't expect to hear from me. He'll call us after I'm back to tell us what he thinks. I'll be back tomorrow night. I have an appointment with my tailor before I come home." He had made the call himself. He wanted to order some new suits. That always cheered him up, even though according to Wendy all his suits looked the same. He favored dark blue and dark gray. They were studio head suits. He thought maybe he'd buy a summer weight too, and a summer blazer.

Violet stood looking dazed as he drove away, and then she rode her bike home and went to bed.

The traffic was lighter than expected, and Andy got to Claridge's at five-thirty. He signed in at the desk, and the assistant managers recognized him immediately. He thought their greeting wasn't quite as warm as usual, but they were busy and he told himself he was imagining it. One of the new younger managers escorted him to his room, which was on the opposite side of the building than he usually liked, but they had a list of his favorite suites so he wasn't concerned.

"We've been remodeling some of the rooms," the

young assistant manager told him, and stopped at a door that didn't look familiar to Andy. He led the way into the room, and Andy saw it wasn't a suite, it was a simple room with a queen-size bed. It had bright, cheery flowered chintzes, but the room was smaller than what he liked, and there was no living room. He turned to the manager and spoke clearly.

"I'm afraid not. This isn't a suite, and it's not on my list of preferred rooms. You'll need to change it immediately. Call the front desk. Now, please." Andy's tone left no doubt in the young manager's mind that there was about to be trouble.

"The house is full, sir," the assistant manager said, almost trembling.

"Fine," Andy said calmly. "You told my assistant I'd have one of my usual suites. If that's not possible, then get me a car to take me to another hotel and get me a reservation somewhere for an appropriate suite. Let's go downstairs, shall we?" There was no doubt in Andy's mind that news had traveled in the last month and crossed the Atlantic that Andy Westfield was no longer the head of Global Studios. His rating had slipped dramatically, and he was clearly no longer on the hotel's prime VIP list. It wasn't a mistake, or about a full house, it was a change of status, and after all he'd been through, Andy was not going to accept being humiliated by the hotel staff too. It was a point of principle for him now.

He asked for the general manager at the front

desk, while three of the assistant managers con-
ferred in panicked whispers, looking frantically at
the computer for another suite, and claimed they
couldn't find one available.

The general manager appeared, obsequious and
professional, and spoke to Andy. There was a stand-
off between the two men, and Andy assured him
it wasn't a problem as long as the manager got him
a suitable suite at another hotel, since Claridge's
couldn't supply one, and he wouldn't be back again,
of course. Miraculously, the general manager discovered that there had been a cancellation only
seconds before for one of Andy's favorite rooms,
and the GM escorted him to the suite himself, and
had a bottle of Cristal in a bucket of ice delivered
to the room. A voice was never raised, and Andy
wasn't rude, but there was no doubt in their minds
now that there would be no change of status for
Mr. Westfield's reservations in future. It woke Andy
up to the fact that he would be facing other situa-
tions like this, probably even more so in LA, where
he was no one now, with no official job and no status. He wasn't the head of anything anymore. He
was the head of Global Studios who had been fired.
It was yet another blow to his ego, and he told
himself it didn't matter, as he sat down and looked
around the room he had fought for. It was a small
victory. In the end, it was just a hotel suite, and he
wondered how many battles like this he was going
to have to fight to prove that he still mattered and

was worthy of respect. And who was he proving it to? Himself? Even without a job, he was a thousand times more important than the hotel clerks and the restaurant waiters and the maître d's who were going to test him and try to bring him down a notch, to make themselves feel important and Andy insignificant. It had come to that. He had won the battle, but wondered if it was really worth it. It depressed him as he took a shower and dressed for dinner with Dash. He was wearing slacks and a blazer and didn't bother to wear a tie.

The doorman nodded when he saw Andy leave the hotel to get in his car, but he didn't rush forward to help him as he used to. It was amazing who needed to make the point, and if Andy became head of another studio by some miracle, would they come running again? Was their obsequiousness the yardstick by which he was supposed to measure his importance in the world? It seemed pathetic, and even more so that he felt it like a blow.

He got into the car the hotel had provided for him, and he gave the driver the name and address of the restaurant.

"Of course, sir," the driver said smoothly as the car left the hotel, and Andy wondered how people knew. Did they put it on a bulletin board somewhere when someone got fired? Or on the internet? It made Andy realize how some women must feel when their husbands left them, and they no longer had the status they'd had for years. He felt foolish that it mattered to him, but the truth was, it did. And back in the world, away from his sleepy little beach town, where he had become a recluse and was hiding, he missed being a man with thousands of employees, on the top of the mountain, running his kingdom, and most of all, he missed being king. It made him feel small and petty to admit it, but he felt like less of a man now without all the trappings of his job. He looked the same, but inside in the deepest part of him, where no one could see it, he felt different, and they knew it anyway. He was different. He no longer had an important job. He was no longer CEO of anything. He was no one now, in their eyes and his own.

He saw Dash waiting at the bar as soon as he walked into the restaurant. Dash looked as unkempt as ever, as though he had slept in his clothes. Andy smiled when he saw him and forgot about the slights he'd just experienced. In the scheme of real life and what was important, it didn't matter. Or he tried to tell himself it didn't.

He and Dash both enjoyed the evening, talking about the movies Dash was making and his plans for the next year, and with the help of the wine, they discussed options for Andy's future, some of which sounded interesting, and many unrealistic. Dash still wanted to talk him into making independent movies, but Andy didn't want to be a producer, with all the details and aggravation and stress it entailed. Dash thrived on it, but Andy felt too old to start all over again. He wanted a ready-made job at the top in a more orderly world. He wanted what he had and lost so swiftly.

"Yeah, but then look what happens," Dash pointed out. "They put you on the hot seat and hit 'eject' and you're out on your ass ten minutes later, with no empire to run. Jobs like you had come at too high a price. They kill you in the end." It was exactly what had happened to Andy. "No one can fire me except myself. I like that better," Dash said, and Andy smiled at his description. "Not to mention the goons who walk you to the curb and leave you there. You're not the only one it happened to, it happens every day," he reminded Andy. Andy knew it was true.

"Maybe I'm too old for the game," he said. "Maybe I should retire."

"Never, that's instant death. You've got great years left in you. You're still young. You're in your fifties. You should try something new. You may like it better than running the world, and risk getting fired if you don't play the politics right. The power game is dangerous, at too high a price. Your ass is on the line every single day." Andy hadn't realized how true that was until now.

"I noticed," Andy said with a rueful smile. He was still licking his wounds from the sudden fall onto cement.

"The industry needs you, Andy," Dash said. "You're one of the smartest guys in it, you've got more integrity than anyone in the business. You're a class act. Don't give it up, just change the game. Do what you enjoy for a change."

"I enjoyed the power game," Andy admitted, after half a bottle of wine.

"It's not worth it," Dash said. "It breaks your heart when it goes wrong. Come have some fun. Let's make a movie together." He desperately wanted to do a project with Andy and had wanted to since they met.

"See what you think of the manuscript I brought you," Andy changed the subject. He liked Dash and didn't want to turn him down.

"I will. I'll call you in a few days, when I've read it. I'm jammed this week."

"There's no rush. It's a beautiful piece of writing, though, and a great story. I think it could be a huge hit with a great screenwriter and the right cast, indie or not."

"The screenwriter is always the problem. It takes six months to find one. They're booked for a year, and they're slow as molasses. They slow me down every time. I have a stable of them, and I still have to wait a year."

"We had a lot more than you do, at Global, but they slowed us down too," Andy admitted. "See how you like her story first, before you worry about a screenwriter." Dash nodded, and they each had another glass of wine before they left the restaurant. Dash went home, and Andy went back to the

hotel. He and Dash had had an honest conversation about the movie industry, and life. Andy was
at a crossroads and still didn't know which way to
go. He was looking for answers, and couldn't find
them, groping his way along in the dark. He felt
lost, and as though aliens had stolen his identity
along with his job.

He had another drink when he got back to his
suite and passed out.

Andy was dressed and ready to leave the hotel at
ten-thirty the next morning. He had an appointment with his tailor on Savile Row at eleven, when
Dash called him. Andy had paid for dinner, and he
assumed Dash was calling to thank him. He was
hungover and suspected Dash was too.

"You owe me one," he said when Andy answered
the phone, and laughed.

"What for? I think we were both overserved."

"I was up all night. I finished the manuscript at
six o'clock this morning. It's a killer piece of work,
you were right. She's a fantastic writer. I love the
story, it almost sounds real. I want to produce it
with you. I'll coproduce it if you will. We could
have a ball with it, with a top-notch cast. Come on,
Andy, let's do it."

"I'll think about it. I'm glad you love it too. You
don't need me." He didn't want to hurt Violet's
chances, but he didn't want to commit to making a

movie in England either. Eventually, he wanted to go back to LA. "How long do you think it would take you?"

"If the stars line up right, with a good cast and director, we could put it all together pretty fast. The plot twists are complicated, and the nuances, but technically it's not. I think we could wrap it up in three months. That's the beauty of an indie. And you wouldn't have to be around for pre- and postproduction, that's all mechanical stuff. You can come and go during the filming, you don't have to be around all the time."

"I know what it takes. It's a big commitment," Andy said seriously.

"Yeah, so what? And a lot of fun. More than you've had in years, probably."

"You may be right." Andy laughed. "Especially lately."

"The problem is going to be the screenwriter, just like we said last night. I only know two people I'd want to give it to who would do it right, and they're booked into the next millennium whenever I call them. I'd have to see who's available. But I want to do it. If you'll coproduce, you've got a deal." Andy groaned when he said it.

"Now you're trying to make me feel guilty. That's blackmail."

"Of course. This is still the movie industry." They both laughed.

"I'll think about it. What kind of money can we

get her for the original story?" He cared about that. He knew Violet needed the money. He hardly knew her, but he wanted to help her, and do a good deed for her, if he could, without sacrificing himself.

"She's hot. And she's going to be big after this. Are you acting as her agent?"

"No, just her advisor." Dash threw out a figure that sounded reasonable to Andy, and he suspected would sound like an enormous fortune to Violet, but this was her first manuscript, and professionally she was a novice, so it was fair in the world of films. She'd get even more for the next one, if she wrote another movie. "She'll have to get an agent and see what they say, but it sounds like a good ballpark figure to me," Andy said. "I'll talk to her. It's a lot to think about."

"I'll see what screenwriters are available. Let's talk in a few days," Dash said. "And thanks, Andy, for bringing it to me."

"Don't make me sorry I did, holding a gun to my head to coproduce." Andy was serious about that.

"You know, we can both afford to put the money in ourselves, and then we own it, and we don't have to screw around with investors." It was an interesting suggestion, which gave Andy even more to think about. "Talk to you soon," Dash said, and hung up. He didn't want to give Andy a chance to turn him down, at least not that fast. He wanted the idea to percolate for a while, and simmer on the stove.

Andy checked out of the hotel and went to his tailor. He ordered three suits, some trousers, and a summer blazer. He was finished at noon, and set off for East Sussex. He had a lot to tell Violet when he got back, and to think about himself. But did he want to coproduce an indie movie? He just wasn't sure. He didn't think so, but Dash made it so tempting. It was a first step back into life. Part of him still wanted to wallow for a while and feel sorry for himself. Producing would be new and fresh and very different. He could do it once, for the hell of it, to make an independent movie. He had nothing else to do. And he respected Dash. People would think he was crazy, producing an indie movie. They had thought his father was crazy when he directed his first picture, and the naysayers predicted it would fail. It had been one of his best films and a huge box office success and had launched a second career for him.

Andy turned the idea around and around in his head, and finally fell asleep in the car. He could hear his father's voice in his head, when he was young, telling him to seize every opportunity with both hands but be smart about it. He wished he could ask him what he meant. Andy had been a screenwriter and then a studio head. And an independent producer of a small film in England? People would think he was nuts. Maybe he was. And maybe, just maybe, being nuts wasn't so bad.

Chapter 9

Andy woke up in the car just as they got to the village. He had slept for several hours and felt groggy, but the headache from his hangover was gone. The past twenty-four hours felt like a dream. He had known that Violet's manuscript was good, but he hadn't been sure what Dash's reaction would be, or if he'd be interested. Andy hadn't expected Dash to go that crazy over it. It was good news for Violet, and he was happy to be the facilitator. He hadn't wanted to be more than that, just the messenger, a benevolent presence to do a good deed for a good woman who needed help and had an amazing talent, and was drowning alone in a backwater, where he had found her purely by chance. Fate was a strange thing, and brought people together who would never have met otherwise.

He saw Violet's bike leaning against the house when they pulled up, and he thanked the driver for the easy journey, and asked him if he wanted to come inside for something to drink before going back to London. The driver thanked him and said he didn't. He was already turning the car around to leave when Andy walked into the house.

He glanced into the study and saw Violet at the desk, frowning as she concentrated on what she was doing. He watched her from the doorway. She was beautiful with her hair loose, intent on her work. She sensed him, looked up, and smiled. He had been an angel fallen from the sky for her. She didn't understand how or why it had happened, but she was grateful. Her deep violet eyes were warm as she looked at him, and he walked into the room.

"Working on the story?" he asked her as he approached. It felt good to be home and he was happy to see her. The house had become home to him very quickly, he was so comfortable, it felt like a safe refuge.

"Answering your correspondence," she said, sitting back in the chair. She was afraid to ask him how it had gone in London, and Andy had warned her that Dash Hemming wouldn't have time to read it right away. He was just delivering it to him, so she didn't expect a response. "I assume you don't want to fly back to LA for the premiere of Alana Beal's new movie." She smiled at him. "Do you know her?"

Andy hesitated and nodded. "We were dating

when I got fired." He noticed that he could say the word out loud now without wanting to cry or feeling sick. It was just a word now. "She disappeared faster than spit in the wind, as my father used to say." He smiled when he said it.

"Nice of her," Violet said with a disapproving look.

"She doesn't do failures. Who she dates is part of her career plan. I haven't spoken to her since the day it happened. She called to say she was sorry, but more or less what she meant was goodbye. I hear she's dating an important director now." Andy didn't believe the rumor Dirk Howard had shared with him that she was dating the new head of Global Studios. Andy knew Alana well. Jeff Latham was married. Alana didn't do scandal. All she wanted was success. Violet looked for signs of sorrow on his face, but there were none.

"Were you in love with her?" she asked softly, and he shook his head.

"It was comfortable and easy. It would have ended soon anyway. She does her job well. We dated for three years, and we had pretty much played it out by then." Violet nodded. "I don't think either of us was ever in love. Dating me was part of her career plan, and for me, it was easy and uncomplicated."

"You live in a hard world."

"We all do. It just comes in different forms, with different faces and costumes. She's an obvious one. The dangerous ones are the ones you don't see coming." Violet looked away and he sat down in

the chair across the desk from her. "I have something to tell you," he said carefully, and she looked
instantly worried.

"He refused to read it and gave it back to you?"
That was the worst case she had imagined, under-
estimating his power again, even now, with no job.

"No. We had dinner last night, and a lot of wine."
He smiled at her. "You kept him up all night. He
read it when he got home. He called me this morning. He loved it, Violet. **Really** loved it. He wants
to do it as a movie." She stared at him, and her
mouth opened slightly and no sound came out as
tears filled her eyes. She wiped them away, embarrassed, and the gesture touched him profoundly.
She was so delicate and so vulnerable, and another
part of her seemed so strong. Without meaning to,
with his unexpected kindness, Andy had gotten behind her walls.

"Oh my God. Now what happens?" she finally said.

"It's a long process. He's going to look for a
screenwriter to turn the manuscript into a screenplay. That's the longest part. It's hard to find good
writers, they're usually booked up for months or
even years, and most of them write slowly and are
finicky. It could take a year or two from now, but
if everything goes well, I think it could happen.
The writing doesn't take as long as finding the right
screenwriter to do it. That's how I started in this
business, as a screenwriter, so I know how long the
process can take. It used to drive me crazy. Dash

Hemming wants to find the right one. He thinks your story is brilliant. So don't get too excited yet. It's a long process. Next, I want to find you an agent, to handle the business end for you and get you the best deal he or she can." He didn't tell her that Dash wanted him to coproduce and was trying to make it part of the deal. He knew Dash would give that up if Andy was adamant about not doing it. Dash wouldn't want to lose a property he considered brilliant, but he would keep the pressure on Andy for a while, and Andy didn't want Violet to worry about it.

"What do I do now? Is there something I have to do?"

"We wait to hear from him. It may be quite some time, while he hunts around for a screenwriter. Months, probably. He may want to option the manuscript, so you don't sell it to someone else, especially if we find an agent for you. It'll give you a little money now if we sell him an option," and he knew she needed it, or could certainly use it.

"It doesn't feel real," she said, still looking stunned.

"The movie business isn't real, but it can be very exciting. And one day you see it on the screen, after all the fighting and crying and negotiating and hoping and worrying and all the work, and it's out there forever, your story on the screen. It is very exciting." He had lived it with his parents and his own career, before he was studio head. Wendy had watched all the movies he'd written. He had done

mostly serious dramas, a few comedies he had enjoyed writing, and his first two movies for his father.
"It's just starting for you, Violet. It may take some
time, but it's going to happen." She could hardly
breathe, thinking about it. "Maybe we should go
to the chippy and celebrate with dinner," he said,
grinning, and she laughed. She was euphoric. It felt
unreal as she looked at him gratefully.

"I don't know how I'll ever thank you enough,"
she said in an awed voice.

"Invite me to the premiere. I'll come to yours."

"I don't know how this happened. You rented
this house and needed help with your emails, and
I forgot my folder on the desk and you read it,
and now we're talking about making a movie."

"That's how it happens in this business—luck,
chance, coincidence, a lucky break. Most of the
opportunities I've had happened that way. It's how
a lot of stars get discovered, and how a lot of great
movies get made. It's a little bit like gambling, rolling the dice. That's what's exciting about it. A lot
of great projects never get completed, so you're already way ahead of the game. Dash is a solid guy,
and if he says he wants to make it, he will, and he
has a solid gold reputation," and she could sense
that Andy did too, and didn't make empty prom-
ises. "What are you going to do to celebrate?"

"I think I'll take a walk on the beach. I need some
air," she said, standing up. She'd been working all
day, and this was an enormous piece of news for

her. She was trying to absorb it. "Do you want to come?" she asked him, and he nodded. It made him think of the day he thought he had seen her on the beach, the day after he arrived, and he thought she was crying. He was sure now that it was her, although she gave no indication of recognizing him when she came to the interview. He wondered if in her tearful grief she hadn't even noticed him on the beach, nor remembered him later.

He was glad to be the bearer of good tidings. His mission had been accomplished, as her random benefactor. A good deed along the way for a good woman who deserved it. It had been easy for him, and he liked seeing Dash and had enjoyed dinner with him, except for the headache that morning.

"I'll get my jacket," he said in response to her invitation to join her for a walk on the beach. There was something so healing about the sea air, the water, and the wind on their faces. It was still chilly in April, and always windy.

He was back a few minutes later in jeans, a sweater, a light windbreaker, and running shoes. She had worn jeans too and running shoes to work and a heavy fisherman's sweater. She didn't think she'd see him when he got back, and hadn't bothered to wear makeup, and had just put her hair into a big clip. She was quiet on the walk to the beach along the familiar path. She had so much to think about, with everything he'd said. She wondered how long it would take Andy's friend to find a screenwriter and wished she could write the script herself, but she didn't know how. The manuscript had been hard enough.

Once they got to the beach, she closed her eyes for a minute and felt the wind on her face. It felt good and clean and blew the cobwebs away, but it didn't make his news seem any more real. They walked silently side by side for a few minutes, each of them lost in their own thoughts. There was a question he had been wanting to ask her, but hadn't dared. But in light of their initial success with this first round, he decided to brave it.

"Violet, you don't have to tell me, but I've been wondering, how much of the story is true?"

"Does it matter?" She glanced at him cautiously and he shook his head.

"No, not technically. I was just curious. Some of it seems so real. Dash mentioned it too."

She didn't answer for several minutes, and he thought she wasn't going to. "A lot of it is," she finally said. "Most of it, but not all. I changed some things and left out others. And the end is entirely fictional."

"It's a great ending," he said. "The whole story is great, and how you laid it out. The tension you built into it is incredible. Dash couldn't stop reading till he finished it. Neither could I." Violet started to walk more slowly as she answered him. There was a faraway look in her eyes, and an expression of bottomless sadness that tore at his heart. They sat down on the tiny pebbles on the beach side by side, close to each other, and she looked out to sea.

"His name was Gabriel Foster. He was a genius and came up with an incredible investment system. People were making money in enormous quantities, and so was he. He made billions, literally. He became a billionaire practically overnight. Everyone in the financial world was talking about it. I was a reporter at **The Sunday Times** then, in my first job, and they assigned me to interview him. He was already living here, in seclusion, and I came to see him. And he was everything people said about him. Gabriel is a genius, truly. He has an incredible mind. He's completely twisted, but you don't see it at first—all you see, and feel, is the amazing charisma. He sweeps you away with him. You believe everything he says. He's like a magnet, drawing people to him. People begged him to take their money and invest it, and he did.

"I wound up staying for the weekend to finish the interview. It was the most unbelievable, magical three days of my life. I went back to London and wrote the article, and my editors were thrilled. I knew every detail about him, or thought I did. Later, I found out that everything he told me about his history was a lie. Eton, Cambridge. He grew up in a slum in Liverpool. He's so convincing, he makes everyone believe him. He'd been married and divorced twice and lied about that too.

"And he came after me then. After I wrote the

article, he pursued me and courted me and swept me off my feet. He was like a tidal wave. He wanted me and he wouldn't take no for an answer. My parents were already dead by then, I have no family, and I had no one to talk to about him. My girlfriends thought he was fabulous, four dozen roses nearly every day, a diamond bracelet, weekends in the South of France, a trip to Italy, another trip to New York.

"One very old editor at the **Times** told me to be careful, that men like Gabriel were dangerous. I thought she was crazy and a bitter old woman. She was right, of course. He was dangerous, but I didn't see it then, or for a long time. I married him four months later, on a yacht he chartered in the Caribbean. It was a fairy-tale ending in my rather mundane life as a junior reporter, with very little money remaining of what my father had left me, and three roommates. I moved down here a few weeks before we got married. He was still putting the finishing touches on the house." She turned to look at Andy then, as he listened raptly and didn't interrupt her. He sensed a frightening tale unraveling, and he had read the manuscript. This had a familiar ring to it. "The house you're renting was Gabe's house. We lived there for eight years. That's how I knew the secret panel in the library." It made sense to him now. He nodded and didn't comment. It was how she knew the housekeeper, who was so fond of her.

"Everything was perfect for the first year. Totally, completely, absolutely perfect. I was madly in love with Gabriel, and he was wonderful to me. The money was rolling in. I never worked with him, so I didn't know how his system worked. He couldn't seem to lose money, only multiply it endlessly. We had security guards to keep people away from the house. He wanted a baby, and so did I, and I got pregnant right away. We had a son, Liam. We both adored him." Andy didn't like the past tense she was using and watched her face closely, but her eyes were softened by the memories she was reliving.

"Everything stayed perfect for four years, or seemed that way. Gabriel isolated me from my friends and said he wanted me to himself. He invested the little money I had left, and of course I lost it like everyone else. He always had a plausible explanation and an excuse. He made every lie seem like the truth. I know he had some sort of business problems after our first four years, but I never knew the details. He went to Malta quite a lot, Liechtenstein, Switzerland, all the places where people hide money, or did then. Some of that has changed. He didn't seem worried, and then I overheard some conversations, and I knew. I figured out that his whole structure and scheme was crooked. It was a scam. Gabe was cheating people out of billions of dollars, smart people with enormous fortunes who gave him millions to invest, and little people who gave him everything they had. That was the worst part of it. Rich or poor, he left them all penniless in the end, including me. Several people committed suicide once he was exposed and they found they had nothing left.

"By our fifth anniversary, I knew Gabe was totally dishonest, a criminal. I confronted him, and I wanted to leave him. He turned into someone I had never known before then. He threatened to kill me and Liam if I exposed him, and I think he would have. He loved our son, but he had too much at stake to let me expose him. Liam was four. I couldn't put him at risk, so I stayed. I had no choice. Gabe went on stealing from people, more and more as he got deeper in. There was some suspicion about him then, but not much, and he always managed to turn it around. I was trapped for three years, knowing what he was, and held hostage to protect our son. He bought a castle in the north of England, and we spent Christmas there. I hated it. It was a depressing place. It snowed and Liam loved it. We built a snowman together, with a top hat." Her voice grew raw as she said it, and instinctively Andy took her hand and held it, to hold her back from the abyss of her memories. He was sorry he had asked her about the story and made her relive it for him.

"Gabriel took Liam out for a drive on Boxing Day, the day after Christmas. They were going to go ice-skating on a frozen pond. Gabe was driving one of his Ferraris, he had many, and he loved to drive fast. Liam loved it too. The car spun on the ice and hit a tree. Gabe hadn't put Liam's seat belt on—he went through the windshield and was killed instantly. Gabe wasn't hurt." She choked on a sob then, and Andy pulled her into his arms and held her as she cried.

"You don't have to tell me the rest," he said gently.

"Yes, I do," she said, sobbing. "I want you to know about Liam. He was such a beautiful little boy and I loved him so much. You asked me if I had children, and I said no. But I did. I had Liam." Andy held her until she could speak again.

"I had nothing to lose after that. Liam was gone, and I didn't care if Gabe killed me. I would have welcomed it. I had nothing left to live for. I went to the police the day of the funeral and told them everything. They believed me. I never went back to him. The police protected me and put me in a safe house. Gabe ran for a while, but they caught him very quickly. It was a huge story in the news for a long time. He went to prison, for forty years. Ten of it is for manslaughter, for not putting Liam's seat belt on. That was three years ago. I hadn't been in the house again until I came to interview with you. I didn't want to be there, but I needed the money and you were so nice, and you seemed in a bad way, and I felt bad for you. I thought maybe you had lost someone you loved too, and then I read on the internet about what happened to you. I never go upstairs, I just stay on the main floor." Andy realized that was true, and he felt terrible about the pain he had put her through just being there. "I can be in the house now, it's okay. I'm better. It's been three years. It always stays with you, but the pain becomes livable. I was lucky to have Liam at all, even for seven years.

"At first, after he died, I wanted to die too. But then somehow, you put one foot in front of the other, you wake up the next day, and another, months go by and then years, and you're still alive and somehow you make sense of it. The time around the trial was awful, and the police could have charged me as an accessory because once I knew that he was a criminal, I didn't report it, but I was his wife, and because he had threatened me and our son, they didn't press charges. I changed back to my maiden name because he was and is the most hated man in England and he hurt so many people. I feel terrible about the people I hurt by not reporting him sooner, but I couldn't risk my son. Once he was gone, I had nothing to lose any-more, so I did. I thought for a while he'd have me killed for exposing him, after he went to prison. The best lawyers in the country couldn't save him, but it would trace too easily to him if he had me killed. He's already in prison for forty years. I sup-pose he doesn't want to make it any longer than it is. I haven't seen Gabe since the day of Liam's funeral. They didn't make me testify at the trial, since I was his wife. But they read my statement, and there were so many others, they didn't need me. Those poor people, thousands of them lost all their money. We lost everything too. But we didn't deserve to have it anyway. I gave them everything, jewelry, most of my clothes, anything that was mine and he'd given me, and they took everything of his. It will all be part of the sale. That's why no one has bought the house in three years. It was all built with ill-gotten gains, and no one wants the association with it. I suppose a foreigner will have to buy it, someone like you." She smiled at him, and wiped away her tears.

"I wouldn't want it either, knowing all this." Andy thought suddenly of the children's toys and furniture he had seen in one of the upstairs store-rooms. They were Liam's. And all of their seized possessions had been boxed up.

"Violet, are you sure you want to sell this story for a movie?" They were still huddled close together on the beach, and he had an arm around her, holding her tight. There was no child in the story she had written. That would have been too much for her. And she had left some other things out, but there were strong similarities to her own story, which was why it was so powerful and so mesmerizing.

"I think I need to tell it. Writing it freed me. I

want to make the movie, and maybe a book from it after that. Can we dedicate the movie to Liam?" she asked quietly, and he held her even closer.

"Of course. I'll tell Dash. Violet, you're the bravest woman I've ever known." She had lived through hell for years with a monster, and an even deeper hell ever since she lost her son. There was no coming back from it. She would never hold her little boy in her arms again. Andy had no idea how she had survived it and was still able to walk and talk and live and breathe and work, and write the story. It had probably been cathartic, but that was small consolation. He was overwhelmed with the enormity of her loss, and suddenly ashamed of how devastated he had been and how sorry for himself over his own losses. He had lost a job, not a child. His ego had been wounded, not his heart. He had never respected anyone more than he did Violet at that moment. They sat together side by side for a long time, looking out to sea, and she rested her head on his shoulder. She deserved all the good in the world now. But no matter what he did to help her, it would never bring Liam back. She had to live with the loss forever.

Andy realized too that he had led a charmed life until now, and nothing bad had ever happened to him, except losing his parents, which had been in the normal order of the universe, and not a tragedy. Violet had been through the worst things anyone could go through: betrayal, terror, threat, fear for her own life and her son's, being hostage to a criminal for three years, and losing her boy. Nothing Andy had experienced even remotely compared to it, and he wished he could make it up to her, but he couldn't, except by being there for her, and doing what he could for her now. It was the least he could do for another human being. They had crossed into different territory that afternoon, and he knew when they stood up and walked back to the house together that he loved her.

Andy drove Violet back to her tiny, dilapidated cottage that night. Neither of them wanted dinner. He hugged her again and she got out of the car. It seemed wrong yet again that she was living in poverty, nearly in squalor, while he was living in the luxury and comfort of her old home. But that house was tainted for her now, and even for him. He was sorry he had rented it, even though it was so comfortable. He hoped it sold so she could try to forget about it. But she seemed to have made her peace with it, although he knew she must have countless memories of her baby there, and the first happy years of her marriage, while Gabriel Foster had still been able to fool her. But the unhappy memories far outweighed the tender ones.

He watched the light go on in her cottage. He hadn't told her about his newborn feelings for her, because it seemed wrong in the context of what she had shared with him, and he didn't want to take advantage of her. He didn't know if the time would ever be right to tell her. But at least he could do whatever he could, and make life easier for her now.

Her story had put his own unhappiness into context. He had lost power, and a job. It had been exciting and exhilarating, even thrilling, and flattering for nineteen years, but it wasn't who he was. His job didn't define him. He felt humbled as he drove back to the house. The house had ghosts in it now for him too, a little boy who had died at seven, his life cut so short, a criminal brilliant to the point of genius who had destroyed countless lives, and one incredibly brave, honorable woman who had managed to survive with unimaginable courage and the love and memory of a little boy. He hated how cruel life had been to her, but maybe he could make it up to her somehow. For now, it was his only goal.

Chapter 10

In spite of the emotional revelations of the day before, Violet came to work on time in the morning. She looked tired when she saw Andy, but she felt totally at ease with him now. He knew all her secrets and had seen the scars, but only saw her inner beauty. She was a shining example to him.

He looked tired too when he met her in the study and smiled at her. He had hardly slept the night before, but he was thinking clearly, and knew what he wanted to do. He needed her agreement and then he planned to call Dash. He still had some qualms about her exposing a story that ran so close to the truth, and someone was bound to make the connection at some point, but she wanted to do it, to honor Liam, and he couldn't argue with that.

He brought her a cup of tea the way he knew she liked it when he came to the study, and stretched out his long legs in one of the big leather chairs when he sat down.

"Thank you for the tea," she said softly. She seemed so fragile, but he knew she was stronger than she looked, stronger than anyone he knew, including himself. "What are we doing today?" she asked him, and he looked serious.

"I'm applying for a job," he said simply.

"You are? Did you have an offer?" She was ready to be thrilled for him. It had only been less than five weeks since he'd been fired, which seemed remarkably quick to her.

"Not yet," he answered. "But I know there's an opening, and I've got the right experience for it."

"As a studio head?" He had told her there were no current openings, but something must have changed. He must have had a call from LA during the night.

"No, better than that." He seemed very sure of himself as he sat straight up in the chair. He seemed powerful again, and not beaten. She had seen the dark side of his despair, but now he had seen hers, and it had renewed his strength. He felt like himself again, a better version of himself, because of her. "I was a screenwriter for sixteen years before I was a studio head, and to be immodest, I was good at it. I wrote some damn good pictures, and I'm fast. Dash is going to spend the next six months or a year chasing screenwriters for you, and then they're going to dawdle around trying to convince us how important they are because they take so long to write the script, and will drive us all nuts waiting for the next page or the next scene. I'm applying for the job. I'd like to give it a shot. I happen to be available." He grinned at her. "I'm willing to work long hours. I have nothing else to do. I think I can do it in a month, and if you don't like it, you can turn me down, and we'll get someone else. I'll even pay for another screenwriter myself if you don't like my work." She stared at him and started to laugh.

"Are you serious?" Violet couldn't believe Andy was willing to do that for her, and he had already done so much, introducing her work to Dash.

"I am. And you're the boss. If you'd like to see samples of my work before you hire me, I can have your LA counterpart go to my storage unit and dig up some of my old scripts and send them to you. And I'm also free. You don't have to pay me. It's a gift. I'm still a member of the Writers Guild, in good standing." He had kept his membership out of sentiment, not because he intended to use it. "Do you want Frances to send some of my old scripts?"

"No," she said immediately. "If you say you're good, I believe you. Why are you doing this for me? You've already done so much."

"Because you deserve having something wonderful happen to you. A run of good luck," he said simply.

"So do you. You've just had a terrible blow."

"Maybe it was for the best," he said quietly.

"Some kind of blessing in disguise. Or a lesson I needed to humble me. I'd gotten pretty big for my boots, maybe the universe decided to take me down a notch, or several notches, or dump me on my head to wake me up. It was a job, Violet. A job I loved, admittedly, but there are more important things in life. You reminded me of that yesterday. And I was happy screenwriting too. It's not a big deal. I have the time, and it would be fun working on it with you. So, what do you say? Am I hired?" He grinned at her and she laughed.

"Of course. What can I do to help?"

"We'll work on it together and I'll show you how it's done. Maybe you'll write the next screenplay yourself, which would make things even easier. I think I'll use the dining room as an office. I need a big board," he described the size with his hands, "like the size of a door, on an easel, and some way I can attach things to it, so I can move scenes around. There's an arc to it. It doesn't flow the same way a book does. You'll see," he said confidently. He hoped that he was still up to it. He hadn't written a script in twenty years. He was hoping it was a skill you didn't lose. He was counting on it. It would be embarrassing if she or Dash hated the end result, but he was willing to take the chance. "I'm going to be asking you how you feel about certain scenes, what you feel the fundamental support structure is and what we can do without. Screenwriters get that wrong sometimes, and then the whole thing falls apart. The support structure is very important, like building a house. Some beams hold the house up, and others are purely decorative. We'll need both." He made the process sound fascinating, and he sent her off in search of the materials he needed and went to call Dash from his upstairs study. It was still early, and he woke Dash up when he called him on his cell. He sounded rough.

"Are you sick?" Andy asked him, worried.

"No. I was overserved again last night. The bartender at my favorite pub has a heavy hand and is a little too generous."

"Watch that," Andy warned him. "I did a bit of that myself in the last month, feeling sorry for myself. I have a proposition for you."

"Since I know you're not gay, and I wouldn't be your type anyway, this must be business. Let me sit up, I was still in bed. What's the proposition?"

"You need a screenwriter. I used to be a pretty decent one before Global Studios made me king. Now that I'm back among the peasants, I want to write the screenplay of Violet Smith's manuscript. I'm fast and I'm good. You can keep looking for one who's currently active, but I'll bet I have it finished before you find anyone who's available. And if you hate what I do, or she does, you can hire whoever you find. I'll pay them out of my own pocket, if you don't like my script. And I'm doing it for free."

"She must be incredible in bed," Dash said,

"if you're doing this for free. And twenty-two years old."

"She's thirty-eight and I've never slept with her, and she's an incredible woman. And you'll figure it out eventually anyway. She was married to Gabriel Foster, if the name means anything to you."

"Holy shit! The guy is a monster. That's why it sounds so real." Dash was bowled over by what Andy said.

"She's left a lot out, but he was the inspiration for it."

"That's incredible. She must have gone through hell with him. I'm sorry to hear it. I assume he's in prison now."

"He was sentenced to forty years. He must have thirty-seven left."

"No one deserves it more than he did. He destroyed the lives of so many people—some of them lost all they had, and they were little people. He was indiscriminate about who he ripped off. There were a number of suicides as a result."

"Apparently. She lost her seven-year-old son because of Foster. She's a brave woman."

"I hope I get to meet her. Are you serious about doing the screenplay?" Dash asked him, wide-awake now, and intrigued by the idea.

"I am. I'd like to give it a try, assuming I haven't lost my touch. I think I can knock it out in a month."

"A month? That would be unbelievable. We can

move forward very quickly if we have a script that fast." Dash thought about it for a minute, but it was an easy decision. "Go for it. We've got nothing to lose. If we're not happy with it, we can still keep looking and stand in line for someone else."

"That's what I think. I really want to do it." Andy already sounded better than when Dash had seen him. He sounded awake and alive, and excited to write the screenplay. And Dash loved the idea, the more he thought about it.

"What about coproducing with me?" he asked cautiously.

"I'll do it," Andy said, and sounded definite about it. He was sure now. Even if it was the only independent film he ever made, it would be an interesting experience, and he could think about his long-term career after. "And I'll cofinance it with you, fifty-fifty," Andy added, and Dash whistled into the phone.

"Shit, we've got a screenwriter, and we don't need outside financing. This sounds like a sweet deal to me. I'll keep my eyes open for a screenwriter just in case, and I'm going to start talking to agents about what actors will be available then. If you get me a script by early June, we could start shooting in August or early September. We'll have a finished picture by the end of the year. The locations aren't complicated. We can use my studio outside London. If by some miracle we finish earlier, we might even be eligible for the Golden Globe Awards and the Academy Awards. Andy, this is going to be a hit, I can feel it!" Andy hoped he was right, and it was going to be a fun process getting there. He was going to try his damnedest to write the best script of his career.

After they hung up, he went downstairs and reported to Violet about the conversation. She was wrestling with a big plank of wood and covering it with felt for the board Andy had said he needed. The property manager had gone to see what they could use as an easel to prop it up on. Violet was excited to hear what Dash had said.

"If we start shooting at the end of summer, early fall, we'll need someplace to stay in London. I have to give this house up in October," Andy said. His lease ended then, and the bank was holding the auction to sell it in mid-October. He thought it was just as well, after all that he knew now.

"How long will we be in London?" Violet asked him, looking worried.

"Dash thinks we could do it in three months if everyone works hard, since the locations aren't complicated, and we'll be in his studio most of the time." Dash had invested in an enormous complex of old warehouses that he'd transformed into studios with sound stages several years before.

"Wow, this is really happening," she said, awestruck again.

"Not till we have a script," he reminded her. "I'm going to start working on it tonight." He had always written best during the quiet hours late at night. But this time, he was going to try working day and night, so he could have a script for Dash quickly. And he wanted to turn out the best script he'd ever written, for Violet's sake.

By that afternoon, they had transformed the dining room into a space that he could work in, and the board was set up on two sawhorses, with something to prop up the back. Violet had gotten him a stack of index cards and colored pushpins, and he had set up his laptop on the dining table, on a pad so he didn't scratch the table. He disappeared up to his study then with a copy of her manuscript, which was fully typed now, and he began dissecting it into numerous scenes, some of which they wouldn't use, and others that he felt were vital to the dramatic scope of the plot.

At the end of the day, he came downstairs to the study to talk to her about the direction he was going. She agreed with most of that, made a few changes that he thought improved the flow of scenes, and mentioned several things that she didn't think were essential to the story. He smiled at her when they finished.

"That's exactly the feedback I need from you," he told her, and she smiled at him.

"It's different from writing a book."

"Everything is visual here. We can't rely on the narrative, and so much will depend on the actors and the director, and what they bring to it.

Sometimes one look is worth a whole scene." She left a little while later, and Andy worked late into the night, identifying key scenes and pulling them out of the manuscript. He tacked some of them to the board, and then rearranged the order of them. He wanted to respect the manuscript, but it would undergo an inevitable transformation from book to screen.

He was already at work in the dining room when she came to work the next day. He was working on his computer and had her print the pages at the end of the day.

"How does this sound to you?" he asked, handing her the pages he'd been working on. She sat down in a chair to read them, and looked impressed when she handed them to him twenty minutes later.

"It's fantastic, Andy."

"It's all coming back to me—it's all about structure, and where you put the scenes, to heighten the tension." He was completely absorbed in what he was doing, and Violet left a little while later and came back to bring him dinner. She had bought sandwiches for him, and a salad. He was staring intently at the board when she returned. "It's not working," he said, almost to himself, as he moved some of the cards around again, and then looked up, surprised to see her there. He had been working so intensely that he didn't even hear her come in. He was completely immersed in her manuscript and the notes he had made to divide it into scenes. She didn't want to disturb him, so she left, and he found the dinner she had left several hours later. He worked until three A.M., and was finally pleased with the order of scenes he had pinned to the board. He had them pinned up with different-colored pushpins to identify which were part of the support structure and were strategically placed, and which they could use as filler. And the highly dramatic scenes were pinned up with a different color. He talked to himself as he looked at the board, ate the rest of his sandwich, and poured himself a beer to celebrate a good day's work.

It was a wonderful feeling writing again, and to feel it start to roll smoothly. He used the same techniques that had always worked well for him, and that he had almost forgotten, he hadn't done it for so long.

Andy worked straight through every day, even on the weekends, and Violet came in and out to bring him food and check on him. And sometimes she sat with him, so he could explain what he was doing and ask her how she felt about it. She very rarely suggested a change, because she liked what he did. He seemed to have an instinct for the storyline, since he knew the original now, and she had told it to him, which brought her manuscript even more to life than before.

He spent the entire month of May working on it, and the time passed quickly. The weather had gotten warm, and he didn't notice. And when he felt stuck, he went for a long walk on the beach, sometimes with Violet and sometimes alone, to talk through where he was going, or just to walk along in silence side by side while he thought about it. She thought it was an amazing process and was fascinated to watch him work.

He typed the scenes up himself and had them in numerical order. Wendy called from time to time to check in and was surprised to hear he was writing a screenplay, but she was relieved that he was doing something and seemed to be enjoying it.

Even Andy realized that it was a healing process for him. Ever since Violet had told him her story, he had felt less sorry for himself, and sometimes not at all. It was two months since he'd been fired, and for the first time he didn't care. He just wanted to finish the script and get it right. Violet helped him do that, and her comments gave depth to what he was writing. She reminded him of details he shouldn't leave out that she thought were important. And he wrote in others to create bridges between the scenes to link them together. There was a constant ebb and flow to it, and she could almost visualize the film when she read the daily drafts of his script.

"The actors will want some of this changed," he explained to her, "if they don't feel comfortable saying something I wrote."

Dash called with big news close to the end of May. "We have our female lead," he told Andy. "Marilyn Gray!" She was a huge hit at the moment, and she'd had a baby and taken a year off. She hadn't signed for anything when she went back to work. She was available, flexible with her schedule, and willing to work on theirs. She loved the whole idea of the story and the personality of the female lead, who fought back when her male counterpart threatened to kill her. "She wants the part, whatever our schedule. She's considering a historical movie that doesn't start shooting till January, and she says she won't sign for anything before that, except us."

It impressed Violet to realize how many component parts there were: all the finances, the insurance they'd need eventually, the cast to line up, the director, the cameramen, the costumes and costumers, all the sound and light technicians, and the script. Dash was handling almost all of it, although Andy would get equal billing as coproducer. He was used to being far up the line at the very top, making the final decisions, now he was down on the ground, in the trenches, working on the script. As the studio head he had had the ultimate control, but as the screenwriter, he had the heart and soul of the film in his hands, and all of Violet's words and emotions to get right and honor what she'd written. But so far, she was pleased with what he'd done, and amazed by his talent.

The final scenes were the hardest to write, and Andy worked closely with Violet on them. He wrote the last two scenes several times, and wasn't happy with them, and then finally they slipped into place, and Andy and Violet both agreed they were perfect. Andy looked at her with a broad grin. It was two o'clock in the morning, and she had stayed at the house to work on the scenes with him. Her hair was piled on her head in a clip, and his was askew after he'd run his hands through it dozens of times while fighting with what they had so far. She was wearing an old sweatshirt, and his shirt was wrinkled with his shirttails hanging loose, and he suddenly knew they'd gotten it right, and they were done.

"We did it, Vi!" he said with a victorious look. "That's it . . . I'm not touching the last scene again, it's perfect."

"I think so too," she agreed, as they sat in the dining room, exhausted.

"You can type it up tomorrow. We are finished." It had taken five weeks, and Andy thought it was the best script he'd ever written. He had twenty years more maturity to bring to the process now, greater insight and deeper emotions. "Dash had better get us a first-class cast and director, I don't want to waste this on a bunch of novices." But he already knew they had a fine actress in Marilyn Gray as their star. She was an extraordinary actress, and although she was young, in her mid-thirties, there was tremendous range to her performances, and a wide variety of roles to her credit. And Dash was in negotiations with a brilliant director who loved the script so far. Henry Mason, the director, was expensive but well worth it if he agreed to do the film.

Andy was excited and needed time to wind down. It was an incredible feeling, knowing that they'd finished. He could hardly wait for Dash to read it.

"Thank you for working so hard," Violet said, looking at him gratefully. "The script is even better than what I wrote."

"No, it's just different. It's what you wrote with all the visuals to go with it. I hope we get the director we want to pull all that emotion out of the actors." What Andy knew of the real story had given the script more color and poignancy, and he had written some terrifying scenes too. It was much harder to do than anything he'd written before, because he cared so much about it, and wanted Violet to love it. And she did. She was too wound up to just go home and go to bed too. Andy opened a bottle of wine, and they sat in the kitchen, celebrating.

He'd had three glasses of wine by the time they finished talking about the script, and she'd had two. "I'm not sure I should drive you home," he said. "And I don't trust you on your bicycle." She wasn't sure she did either. She had a slight buzz from the wine, exhilaration, and fatigue. "Do you want to stay here tonight, in one of the guest rooms?" She hadn't been upstairs or slept there since she lived there, and he was afraid it might be a bad déjà vu for her, but an accident on her bicycle would be too.

"I guess I could," she said hesitantly. The alternatives didn't seem wise to her either. "It's been a long time. I have to get past it," she said bravely. The worst had happened at the castle Gabriel owned, and that had been taken away from him too, just as the house in Winchelsea Beach was. The castle had sold quickly. Everything he owned had been purchased with money he had cheated people out of. His victims had gotten some money back, but pathetically little.

Andy and Violet left their glasses and the wine bottle in the kitchen, with barely a drop left in it, and left everything as it was in their respective offices, the library and dining room, and walked up the stairs together, with a feeling of elation, having finished the script.

"I'll sleep in the yellow room," she said with a yawn. It was the room next to his. And he headed to his dressing room to brush his teeth and undress, and gave a start when he saw her standing in the doorway, looking embarrassed. Her hair was loose and tangled. And he had his shirt off and was just wearing his jeans.

"Can I borrow a pajama top?" she asked shyly, and he put his toothbrush down and smiled at her.

"You could if I owned one. How about a shirt?" He took a perfectly ironed blue Hermès shirt off a rack and handed it to her. She looked so fragile as he stood looking at her, he didn't want to frighten her or take advantage of her. She felt odd being upstairs with him, in what had once been her bedroom. "Are you going to be okay, Vi?" She nodded and without even meaning to, he put his arms around her and kissed her. He couldn't stop himself. He had known for over a month that he was in love with her, and had done everything he could not to show her. She was nineteen years younger and had been through so much, but she was kissing him back, with her delicate hands touching his chest, which sent shivers through him.

"I'm sorry, Vi," he said in a hoarse voice when they stopped kissing.

"I love you," she said simply, and reached up to kiss him again. It was more than he could resist, and he followed her to the bedroom next to his and closed the door behind them. They were on the bed together an instant later, their clothes on the floor in a heap, their hunger for each other insatiable. It didn't matter who they were or where they'd been or what they'd done, their bodies and souls merged instantly and they lay as one, swept away on the tides of the passion that had been drawing them together since they'd met. Inexorably, unavoidably, irresistibly, it had been the only possible outcome right from the beginning. Andy felt as though he had come here to meet her, and she had come back to this house of sorrow to find love and joy again.

They were both breathless when their lovemaking ended, and she clung to him as he held her.

"Are you okay?" he whispered in the room lit by

moonlight, and she smiled and nodded. "I love you. Are you okay with this?" He didn't want to upset her, but she was smiling in the moonlight.

"I love you too. This is the way I wanted the story to end." She couldn't stop smiling as he held her.

"Me too. I thought I was too old for you, and I didn't want to take advantage of you," he whispered.

"You didn't." She giggled. "I didn't really need the shirt, I sleep naked." He laughed out loud then.

"You little minx. And you got me drunk!" They both laughed then, and neither of them was drunk as he pulled her closer and they made love again. The script was finished, and their story had just begun, whatever their jobs, or lack of them, or histories. Their time had come.

Chapter 11

Violet wore Andy's shirt with her jeans the next morning, and they both looked like guilty children when Mrs. MacInnes showed up for work. She made no comment, but there was just the smallest hint of a smile on her lips when she asked them what they wanted for breakfast. She could figure out what had happened before she saw the yellow bedroom, and the bed in the master suite Andy hadn't slept in. He had thought of opening it and rumpling the sheets a little before they went downstairs and decided not to bother. They were both single adults and free to do what they wanted. And Violet had the distinct impression that Mrs. MacInnes was happy for them. The housekeeper had hated Gabriel when she worked for him and Violet, and thought that Andy was a fine man, and would be good to Violet. She knew firsthand that Violet had been to hell and back.

*   *   *

Andy called Dash after breakfast and told him he'd finished the script.

"You weren't kidding when you said you're fast."

"It looks a mess. I made some of the changes by hand, but I can send it to you digitally."

"That would be great."

Violet sent it to him a few minutes later, and Dash called them two hours later, stunned.

"You nailed it, Andy. It's the best damn script I've seen in years. You've been wasting your time in that fancy office of yours at Global. You should go back to screenwriting. It's fantastic. We're in. We are all in. I've got a list of possibilities for the cast. I'll send it to you and we can talk about it. The director told me yesterday he'll do it and wants approval of the cast, which I said we'd give him. I'll start making calls as soon as you approve the list. I want to start shooting at the end of August. We should be able to get all the cast contracts signed in the next few weeks. Everyone on the list is available." It was happening. They had done it. Violet's movie was going to be made.

Violet went home to change clothes after breakfast, and she came back in a pretty blue cotton flowered summer dress.

"We have to go to London, you know," Andy said to her, and she looked panicked. He kissed her as soon as she walked in the door. "And by the way, I love your dress." She looked young and feminine, and she'd worn her hair down, which he liked best, but had never dared say to her before. A whole new vista had opened up in front of them after the night before.

"Why do we have to go to London?"

"Because you need to be part of the process. Cast auditions. Meetings with the director. I want you on set when they shoot the movie. This is our project. I want us to do it together," he said, and looked at her proudly. "And you need to meet Dash. We're in business together now. Why don't you want to go?" He could easily sense her resistance, she looked terrified every time he mentioned London to her.

"Because at some point someone is going to remember something or recognize me, and Gabriel's whole nightmarish mess will be all over the press again and it will be an embarrassment to both of us. And I don't want you to be ashamed of me." She had tears in her eyes, and he put his arms around her. He could feel her trembling.

"I'm proud of you, Vi. Nothing could make me ashamed of you. And that's his mess, not ours. You were married to a terrible guy, a criminal. He hurt a lot of people, including you. You had nothing to do with it. And if it winds up all over the press again, I don't care. Look at what you're facing with me, someone is going to say that I'm a has-been, I'm all washed up and unemployed."

"That's crazy, you just wrote a fantastic movie."

"So did you. And Dash already knows about

Gabe. I told him. I thought it was better, in case he heard about it later. He felt bad for you. He didn't think less of you for it."

"It was such a nightmare in the press when it was happening. I don't want you to have to live through that."

"It wasn't so pretty when I got fired either. The press and the tabloids love writing about bad news and making it sound even worse. Most people know that. We're together now, and we're going to make a spectacular movie. I'll be with you. It'll do you good to get out of here. When was the last time you left this place?"

"Three years ago, for the trial. I didn't testify. But I was there, in a private room."

"Let's go have some fun." He smiled at her. "And we have to sign our contracts with Dash."

Violet reluctantly agreed, and a week later they went to London to sign their contracts and watch some of the auditions. His contract and the dates were carefully worded so as to respect the non-compete clause in his exit package with Global. Andy liked the entire list of actors and actresses that Dash had put together, with the exception of one British actor who had given them problems at Global, and Andy didn't want to risk it again. The actor was known to be litigious and had broken a contract with Global. The other actors all had good reputations and were fine performers, and the director was pleased with them. Andy had had several of them in his films at Global, and he knew of all of them. And once she was there, Violet was excited to meet them, and had definite preferences once she saw the auditions. There were roles for both British and American actors, and for actors who could adapt to the accents of their parts.

Andy and Dash signed their contracts with each other as coproducers, and financial agreements to share the cost of the film equally. Violet signed a contract for providing the original story. And Andy signed an additional one as screenwriter. Legally, everything was in order, and Violet was delighted with the amount they paid her. Everyone was happy, and Dash couldn't believe his good fortune to have talked Andy into it.

"You watch. You'll be begging to do the next one. I won't be able to get you off my back. You're going to want to be an indie producer from now on. Fuck the studios." But there were no jobs available to Andy as the head of a studio anyway. Those jobs opened up very rarely, and Andy knew all the players in Hollywood. None of the other studio heads was going anywhere. He couldn't imagine a place opening up for him ever again. His options seemed very limited. He could produce another indie film or retire, which didn't appeal to him at all at fifty-seven. But he wasn't sure yet if he wanted to make another movie. He wanted to see how this one did first. He didn't want to add another failure to his record now, although he couldn't imagine the movie doing badly, the way they were putting it together, with an exceptionally strong cast, and his good script, and Henry Mason as their director.

Andy and Violet stayed in London for two weeks, until the final cast choices were made and all the actors they'd chosen had accepted their roles. They were all willing to start shooting at the end of August. Andy and Violet had lunch with Marilyn Gray, which was a thrill for Violet. Andy had worked with her before, and Dash knew her well. Violet was enormously impressed by her. Andy thought Violet was infinitely more beautiful. And Henry Mason was bowled over by Violet's story and Andy's script. They had a strong rapport.

Andy and Violet went out to dinner every night to trendy restaurants with delicious food, and had dinner at Dash's favorite pub with him twice. They stayed at Claridge's, and got Andy's favorite suite after the fuss he made before. People didn't fawn over him as they used to, but he found it was easier not to have to deal with that, and he liked it better this way. The service they provided was good enough without excess. And he took Violet to Paris for a day of shopping, which she loved. She spent a little of the money she'd just made, and let Andy buy her a pair of shoes at Chanel, and a bag at Dior, but nothing else. She was an entirely different breed of woman from the ones he was used to since his divorce.

He had told Wendy about the film, and he wanted

to visit her sometime before shooting started, but her children were enrolled in camps in July and August and they were busy in June until then, so it didn't work. He had mentioned Violet to her, in discreet terms, and Wendy wasn't surprised that he was involved with someone. He always was, but he told her that Violet was different. Wendy wasn't sure she believed him. Serious, admirable women were not his style. And she thought it was much more likely that he'd have an affair with one of the actresses in the movie. Wendy was surprised that he had actually written the screenplay for an indie film, even if Dash Hemming was a respected producer, but she was relieved to hear her father sounding happy, and not as crushed as he had been three months before. His time in England had been good for him, and she assumed the movie and the new woman were part of it.

Andy had heard from Frances too. She had just taken a job with a famous novelist, and she loved it.

After almost three weeks in London, settling all the details and legal aspects of the film, Violet was almost sorry to leave. She had forgotten how much she loved London. There was so much to do there, and being in the big city was exciting.

Before they left, Andy made her look for an apartment with him. They needed a place to stay during the filming, and Andy didn't want to live in a hotel for three months, or longer. He wanted something homier, and he and Violet looked at furnished apartments and found one in Notting Hill. The current tenant was leaving on the first of August, so they rented it for four months. They both liked the area, and Andy thought it would be fun to be somewhere livelier, instead of Knightsbridge or Claridge's. Dash lived near the apartment they rented. Andy could predict many long drunken nights with Dash at his favorite pubs. They were the mainstay of his social life.

Violet enjoyed everything they did, and they even went to a few museums and got to play tourist between meetings, and when all the business was wrapped up, they went back to Winchelsea Beach. The trip to London had been a big success, and they couldn't wait to start the movie. She was going to live with him in the apartment in Notting Hill during the filming. Andy hadn't lived with a woman since he was married, a dozen years now. He wanted Violet to stay with him at the beach now too. That had been a bigger decision for Violet, given her memories there, but she gratefully agreed. She was going to move some clothes in that weekend. Violet had loved traveling with Andy and couldn't wait to do it again.

"You saved me," Andy said to her quietly on the drive home. "I probably would have been in rehab by now, or seriously depressed. I was heading there when I met you." He still shuddered at the memory of his final minutes at Global, Tony coming to his office to fire him, and being escorted out by security. It was a vision he couldn't get out of his head. And how desolate and destroyed he had felt afterward.

"And I had twenty pounds left in my purse and nothing in the bank when you hired me. We saved each other," she said gently. "And the movie saved us. I want to do another one."

"You haven't even done the first one yet." He laughed at her. "You greedy girl. Wait a while. Let's see how the first one does at the box office."

"I don't care. I want to do another one," she said, sounding like a child. "I love working with you."

"Well, you can still do my correspondence if you want."

"I was expecting to." She looked surprised.

"With frequent breaks upstairs, I hope," Andy said sternly. They were moving into the guest bedroom they had used before. Violet had said she could never stay in the master bedroom again, and he understood why.

He wanted to take her to Capri, Venice, and Portofino in August before they started shooting. He wasn't worried about meeting Hollywood people there. He wouldn't suggest the Hotel du Cap to her, where the Hollywood set went regularly. They would be there in force, and he didn't feel ready to face them yet, no matter how happy he was with their little indie movie. None of them would understand that and would think he had lost his mind. In their opinion, it was far beneath him after being studio head.

They wouldn't see it as an opportunity to be creative, just pathetic, and an object of pity. They wouldn't value the artistic and entrepreneurial benefits. Andy saw all the merits of it, and the fun of working with Violet on new projects. It had brought him out of his slump after being fired and had used skills he had once thoroughly enjoyed that had lain dormant for twenty years. He had loved the challenge of reviving his screenwriting skills, and the results had been rewarding, even before they made the movie. Working on it had already turned his life around, and he felt he owed that to both Dash and Violet and was grateful to both of them. The best was yet to come when they made the movie. But he had loved the work so far.

Violet and Andy went back to their previous habits in Winchelsea in July, working together in the morning, walking on the beach in the afternoon. The town was a little livelier with the arrival of summer renters, but barely. The place was so long forgotten and unpopular that Andy and Violet hardly noticed the summer visitors. Andy had come to love the peace, and the lack of anything Hollywood-related. Neither of them was at any risk of running into the press or being discovered, which was what had drawn Andy there in the first place. It had served its purpose.

He and Violet cherished their time together now, knowing they would be going to London soon, where they would lose their anonymity and their privacy. With Andy's rented house going up for auction while they worked on the film, he wouldn't have it to come back to when filming was over, which made it seem more special now, despite Violet's unhappy history in it. Even she would be sad to leave, and her cottage was too small for the two of them. They would have to figure out a new location for their life together after the movie. Although they enjoyed visiting London, neither of them wanted to live there.

Andy's enormous, spectacular house in Bel-Air was standing empty while his life was seemingly on hold. The people he knew in Hollywood had no idea where he'd gone, and they easily imagined him too embarrassed to show his face, which had been true when he left, but was less so now. He was no longer ashamed. He had just removed himself, and had no desire to go back yet. He wasn't sure if he ever would. The future remained uncertain, but the present, with Violet, had many virtues. He was happy staying out of sight, away from the Hollywood gossip mill, and he wanted to protect her from it now too. He didn't miss anything about it.

*   *   *

Their trip to Italy in August was idyllic, staying in a quaint hotel he had stayed in years before. Capri was fun and crowded. Violet and Andy wandered in and out of the shops, lay by the pool, avoided as best they could the hordes of tourists who poured off the cruise ships that stopped there. They liked getting lost in the crowd, and Andy rented a boat they spent the day on. It was so far removed from their normal lives that it was like being on another planet.

He had always loved the mysteries of Venice. Much to his surprise, Violet had never been there. They visited countless churches, saw the glass factory in Murano, went to all the tourist places, ate gelato in Saint Mark's Square, and stayed in a fabulous suite at the Cipriani across the lagoon from Venice. They rode in a gondola under the Bridge of Sighs, and he bought her a simple gold bracelet that she loved. She was the easiest woman to please that he had ever met, and had few material desires. Those she did have she didn't expect him to satisfy. She just enjoyed being with him, and loved him as he was, which was a new experience for him. The material excesses she had had with Gabriel had no appeal for her. On the contrary, they repelled her, and reminded her of him.

They were sorry to leave Venice after four days, and their last stop on their Italian trip was Portofino, a charming port town, with a medieval castle lit up at night, a beautiful church, a wonderful hotel where

they stayed, the Splendido, appealing shops, a harbor full of boats of all sizes, and beaches nearby.
Violet hadn't been there either and loved it. Yachts
came and went all summer, and it was a favorite
holiday spot to visit for Italians and Europeans.

Andy had his arm around Violet as they came
out of one of the small luxurious shops on the
port, when he bumped into a tall, statuesque blond
woman with a striking figure and found himself
face-to-face with Alana. He was so startled that he
didn't react for a minute, and she looked shocked
to see him, and instantly uncomfortable. She was
with a rival studio head, and he was sure they had
come off one of the yachts in the port, or anchored
just outside the harbor. He had been there himself on yachts that he had chartered. Alana looked
better than ever, and the man she was with was
unattractive, and in his late seventies, but he was
unquestionably one of the most powerful men in
Hollywood, especially with Andy no longer on
the scene. He might have been a step in the power
game she played so well, but not in the scheme of
life, and Andy felt sorry for her. She took ambition
to dizzying heights, and was the exact opposite of
Violet, to whom that game meant nothing.

"Hello, Alana," he said calmly, once he regained
his composure. "How are you? You're looking
well." He thought he saw her nearly blush, and
she looked extremely uncomfortable. She was
wearing a Chanel jogging suit with an oversized

beige alligator Hermès Birkin handbag, which he realized must have been a recent acquisition, and cost someone a fortune. It was hard to believe that he had only been gone for four months. It felt like four centuries. He introduced Violet, who knew instantly who Alana was in the movie world and how she had abandoned Andy the day he was fired. Alana ignored Violet as though she weren't standing next to them, and her escort wandered away, not interested in who she was talking to. He hadn't noticed Andy, but probably wouldn't have stuck around anyway.

"**Where** have you been?" she asked him, as though she'd been expecting him home for dinner every night for the last four months and he hadn't shown up. He'd had no texts, emails, or messages from her since the fateful day.

"I've been in England, working on some projects." He smiled at Violet as he said it, and he felt calmer and more sure of himself with her beside him. Seeing Alana didn't warm his heart, and even chilled him a little. Her defection had been so complete and so immediate. She had been one of the first to get in the lifeboats and leave the sinking ship, and had made no pretense about it. She looked more affected to see him than he was to see her. He had nothing for which to reproach himself. She did.

"Are you coming back to LA?" she asked, as

though she wasn't sure if he'd be useful again and wanted to know how to categorize him.

"Eventually. You know how the industry is. It's built on shifting sands, you never know who'll be up or down or in or out. I'm enjoying life right now, waiting to see what comes." He sounded relaxed about it, and surprisingly he was. He had dreaded seeing her again, and now face-to-face with her, he found it didn't matter.

"Are you working on anything big in England? A series?" she asked pointedly. He remembered how badly she wanted a series to bolster her slowly deflating career, given her age.

"Some interesting projects," was all he would say, with another smile at Violet. "Nice to see you," he said, and with that he put his arm around Violet again, and made his way around Alana, like a rock in a stream, and walked away, while she stared after him. She frequently wondered if she had reacted too quickly. Andy was resourceful, and young enough, he might bounce back one day. She knew her reaction had been hasty. She didn't like wasting time with people who weren't useful to her. Andy had ceased to be the moment he left Global.

"She's beautiful," Violet said in hushed tones once they were out of earshot, and Andy noticed the enormous yacht that had pulled into port while they were shopping, and was sure she had come off that one.

"There's not an inch of the original model on that chassis," he said with a grin. "You're a hundred times more beautiful, and you're real. She's glamorous, but there's not much of a human being in there."

"Her boyfriend looks a hundred and twelve years old," she said with an evil giggle, and he laughed.

"I hope you don't say that about me one day. He's a very powerful studio head. That's why she's with him, not for his good looks."

"I thought you handled it beautifully," she complimented him. "I don't think I could have done that."

"Yes, you could. I had you standing next to me. You made me brave." She was ten years younger than Alana, a thousand times the woman, and he loved her. And he knew that she loved him. He and Alana had never been in love.

"You make me brave too," she said, tucking a hand into his arm. "I think you made her nervous that you have some big deal cooking in England." He laughed out loud.

"I did it on purpose. I couldn't resist. I knew it would panic her that she had bet on the wrong horse. It serves her right. I'm glad you caught that. I hope she did too."

"She looked panicked," Violet confirmed, smiling.

"I doubt that," he said with a satisfied smile. "Alana doesn't do panicked."

"Why not?" Violet asked.

"Too much Botox." They both laughed and

walked into a gelateria to buy ice cream cones, as Alana scurried up the passerelle of the yacht she came in on, feeling slightly sick to her stomach. She didn't like making important enemies, and she wondered if she had one now. She didn't. Andy didn't care about her enough to hate her. It was worse than that. He was completely indifferent, as he and Violet ate their ice cream cones and continued shopping.

Chapter 12

Andy packed everything he'd brought with him to take to London. He still had the house in Winchelsea Beach until the seventh of October, but he didn't know if he'd have time to come back while they were shooting the movie. It seemed simpler to take everything with him. He could use the house if they got a few days off and he wanted to get out of London. Violet took everything she thought she'd need for three months of shooting, and left the rest at her cottage. Andy rented a van with a driver to take them to London.

They were both excited to start work on the movie. They had readings with the actors for the next two days. Andy had a double role as screenwriter and coproducer, which would keep him busy. Violet was going to be an observer to make sure that they didn't stray too far from her original story, and that the actors didn't put a different

spin on it. It was going to be her first time on a
movie set.

Andy had said a warm goodbye to Mrs. MacInnes
and had given her a large tip. She was very pleased.

"Good luck to both of you," she said, looking
emotional, and she hugged Violet. "You both deserve it. You're good people." She too had been
heartbroken when Liam died, having babysat for
him several times. She stood and waved as the van
pulled away, and Brigid joined her. Mrs. MacInnes
was going to live with her sister in Hampshire when
the house sold. She was already packing. The auction was in six weeks. It had been a bad luck house
for Violet, and she would be happy to know that it
was gone forever. It had been a fluke that she had
come back to work there, when the bank sent her
to Andy, which had turned her whole life around,
but she didn't credit the house for that.

"I have an idea for a new story," she said to him
insistently on the drive to London.

"I keep telling you, you have to finish one project
before you start another one. That's how it works,"
he said, amused at her enthusiasm.

"Why? I have a good idea." Violet looked like a
young girl to him sometimes, and he loved her in-
nocence. Given all she'd been through in her life,
she was surprisingly trusting and naïve, and he loved
that about her. There was no anger or bitterness in
her. She wasn't vengeful. She was just a survivor
and her own strength and dogged determination

had gotten her through the hard times. Her quiet perseverance gave him strength for his own life. It was really because of her that he was about to make his first independent movie. He wasn't sure if it would prove to be a blessing or a curse, but he was about to find out.

They settled into the flat in Notting Hill that night, and Andy commented that their belongings seemed to have grown while they were in the van. The flat had a large, airy bedroom, a small guest room, an office, and a big living room with well-worn, comfortable couches and big inviting chairs and a fireplace. It looked like a good spot to gather and there was adequate space for both of them, though far less than the house they had just vacated.

Andy found Violet in the study they would use as an office, later that evening, with a cup of tea, writing frantically in a spiral notebook.

"What's that?" he asked her, and she grinned guiltily.

"Our next movie," she said, and he laughed.

"You're incurable."

"I don't want to forget my ideas while they're fresh in my mind."

"Something tells me that won't happen." He loved how full of ideas she was, how creative and enterprising. She inspired him to work harder.

"Will you do the screenplay again?" she asked him.

"Call my agent," he said, and sat down on the arm of her chair and leaned down to kiss her. "Have I told you today that I'm crazy in love with you?"

"You might have." She smiled at him. "But I like hearing it again."

"Come on," he said, pulling her out of her chair, "I think we should check out the bedroom."

"Why? Is there something wrong with it?"

"You tell me, after we try it out," he said, and she laughed, understanding what he had in mind. She raced him to the bed then, and he fell onto it next to her, laughing. She was so small and delicate that he worried about crushing her sometimes, but she was sturdier than she looked, and not as fragile as she seemed.

He made love to her with sensitivity and passion, and they were both out of breath afterward. He kissed her again and smiled at her.

"I think the bed is okay." He grinned.

"So are you." She laughed. "Maybe we should check it again."

"Only if you want to kill me. I'm not a kid, you know."

"You are to me." She put her arms around him and kissed him, and he was startled to realize that he wanted to make love to her again, and was able to. She was good for him in every possible way. She made him feel like a man again, and not just a bank. She loved him for who he was, not the job he had. She loved him even though he had been fired and reduced to rubble five months ago. His power meant nothing to her. It was his heart she cared about, his soul, his kindness to her, and his talent, that he was only just rediscovering. She made him a better person than he was on his own. She was everything he had ever hoped for in a woman and never found, even when he was young. She was what his mother had been to his father. She was the life force and the energy that fueled him now. He made love to her again, and then he gently pulled her out of bed and told her he was starving.

"If you expect me to make love to you three times a day, you'd better feed me. I saw a chippy down the street. I need food immediately." They took a shower together, threw clothes on hastily, and went to the fish-and-chips restaurant down the street, and agreed that it was a good one.

Violet and Andy slept like happy children in each other's arms that night, and were at Dash's studio the next morning for the cast readings. It was a chance for each of the actors to comment on the script, and request any changes they felt worked better for them. The director would be there, and Andy had to be, to approve any changes they wanted to make. There were already a few ridiculous ones. He hadn't been to a cast reading in years, and Violet said it sounded like fun. Everything she did with him was fun to her. He didn't make up for what she had lost, and he couldn't replace the little boy she'd lost three years before, but he filled her heart as no one else ever had, and she was happy and at peace with him, just as he was with her. He still missed his job as studio head at times, but being with her was a whole new path in life for him, and going back to screenwriting again, with more maturity and freshly honed skills. He was happy. They parked the car he'd rented in the parking lot, and walked into the building where they'd be working together. Andy gave Violet a quick kiss before they walked into the conference room where they'd be meeting with the cast, and he smiled at her.

"Thank you for putting me back to work," he whispered to her.

"Thank you for giving me my life back," she whispered. "A new life," she said more precisely.

"For both of us," he said, and followed her into the conference room where the cast was waiting, with Dash and the director. They took their seats and Dash introduced them all around. Many of the actors were well known and didn't need an introduction, but Dash introduced them anyway. They were all equal here, and for the next three months, they'd be a family. Violet smiled as she looked around the room. They were the people who were going to bring her story to life, and when Dash introduced her, she thanked them, and they all gave her a round of applause, as Andy looked at her proudly.

The filming of their movie was about to begin. They had called it **Tightrope.** He was now the coproducer of a little indie movie. If anyone had told him that six months ago, he'd never have believed them.

Chapter 13

The shooting of Violet's movie was the most exciting time in her life. The cast became exactly what Dash had predicted they would, a family. There wasn't a lemon in the bunch. The women formed a very congenial group, on and off the set, and the actors Dash had hired and Andy had approved were lively and fun, and organized soccer matches among the cast and technicians, and even pulled Andy and Violet into them. There was a cohesive spirit that Andy had never seen on a set before. Dash ran his movies like a loving father. Everyone wanted the film to go well. Everyone wanted to prove that an indie film could be as good as, or better than, a studio picture. The actors helped each other with their lines. They skipped days off to keep the shoot moving. Henry, the director, was brilliant and supportive. One of their goals was to have the film in theaters in the States in time to qualify for both the Golden Globes and the Academy Awards, so time was of the essence. No one wasted time or money. Their talent was abundant, and the story itself was so exciting and the screenplay so tight that it made shooting easier. No one needed twenty takes to get a scene right because they didn't know their lines. They were talented, disciplined professionals who gave it their all and gave stunning performances. And the filming went faster than they'd expected.

It was one of the most exciting productions Andy had ever seen made, and Violet was in awe of what she saw the cast and crew do on set every day. She made very few corrections, only if she felt they were going in the wrong direction, and when she did, they were agreeable about it. Andy worked with the actors when they wanted script changes, and the director brought out the best in them. It was an exciting production for everyone involved. Dash had made an excellent distribution deal in both the UK and the States, which was going to help make the film a box office success.

Andy realized now how good Dash was at what he did. He had always thought so, and respected him, but his admiration grew day by day for the quality of Dash's work, and his sensitivity to the material they were shooting. It was a top-flight production in every way, and Andy was proud to be associated with it. There was no shame in being involved in an independent production like this one. It was a jewel of a movie, and working on it brought Andy and Violet closer with each day and scene that passed, particularly since he knew it was in great part her story.

Word eventually leaked out somehow. It always did on a set, where there were no secrets about anyone or anything, but word spread quietly that Violet was the ex-wife of Gabriel Foster, the criminal who had bilked people out of billions of dollars, and there were whispers that Violet had even lost her seven-year-old son during that time. Compassion and sympathy for her were overwhelming, and the cast and crew were proud to dedicate the film to her son's memory.

The more internationally famous actors were also aware of Andy's previous position with Global Studios, had worked for him before, and quietly expressed their regret to him that he had been dealt such a tough hand and let go.

Godfrey Hunt, the male lead, was particularly kind to Andy.

"It teaches you a lot about yourself, and what matters to you," Andy said to him. "I got addicted to the power game. It's a very dangerous drug. And from one minute to the next you're stripped of everything you thought was so important, and you have to build your whole life over again. You wind up standing naked on the sidewalk, and your whole world is upside down. Your friends don't want to know you anymore, and were never your friends in the first place. The people you trusted betray you, your girlfriend or your wife is gone before the day is out. I came to England to run away and hide, and ended up reviving a skill I had shoved in a drawer and forgotten about for twenty years, screenwriting, which I used to love. If Dash weren't such a stubborn guy, I'd never have made this movie. And I met a woman who taught me what courage really is, and what does matter, not the crap and the tinsel and the phony bullshit. She taught me about being real, and you come back from something like this a different person, a better person than you were. I don't think I was even happy when I was head of the studio. I thought I was. But I was missing out on everything that mattered. I missed my daughter's teenage years and my wife left me, and I was so numb and self-involved that I'm not sure I even cared. The women I dated just wanted a better part in their next movie. They were beautiful and looked great on the red carpet, but none of their moving parts were real. They weren't real. I wasn't even real. But the perks were fantastic. I have two Bentleys and a classic Rolls in my garage, and the biggest house in Bel-Air. I haven't seen the house in six months, and I'm not sure I will again. I'm living in an apartment in Notting Hill with shabby furniture, and I'm happy. It wasn't fun when it happened, but in a way, I recommend getting kicked out on your ass once in a lifetime, so you get to know yourself, what you want, and who you are and what matters to you. In fact, I'm still trying to figure it out. I'm still a work in progress," he said good-naturedly, and every single member of the cast admired him for what he said, and the example he set them, of courage, patience, and determination in the face of adversity.

And he was well aware that at night, like a little mouse, Violet was scribbling away on what she hoped would be her next movie. And he was beginning to hope it would be too.

He was checking in with Wendy regularly. He felt terrible that he hadn't seen her or her kids since February, during a long holiday weekend. He wanted to, but he had gotten so caught up in running away and surviving what had happened and now with the new movie that he hadn't gotten to New York to see them. Wendy and her family were busy and had their own plans too. He had promised he would be there for Thanksgiving, which wasn't easy either, since it wasn't a holiday in England. He had already told Dash that he would have to be away that weekend, without fail. It would have been nine months then since he had seen his daughter, and she was so good about it. She and her family were going to South America with Peter's parents for Christmas, so he wouldn't see them then.

He had asked Violet to join him at Wendy's for Thanksgiving, which was a first. He had never asked any of the women he dated to go to Wendy's with him, and most of them wouldn't have wanted to go. If there wasn't a red carpet involved, Alana had no interest. But Violet wasn't just a date. He felt as though he had found his soul mate and wanted her to meet his family. He only had Wendy and her husband and children. Violet had no family at all, but she didn't want to intrude on Andy's at a holiday occasion as a stranger, and he hadn't seen his family in many months. She told him she'd rather meet them at a less intimate time, which he thought was typical of her, always sensitive to others' feelings. She didn't want to take away Wendy's precious time with him, but he wanted them to meet.

Wendy was curious about her too. He had mentioned Violet several times, which was new for him. His emotions were more raw and open than they had ever been, and there was something different in his voice when he talked about her. All she knew was that her father had hired Violet as an assistant in the small town where he was living, and now he was working on a movie with her. And she had guessed that they were living together, another first for him.

"Is this serious, Dad?" she had asked him. "It's beginning to sound like it. You're spending a lot of time with her."

"That's true, I am. It might be serious. She's an exceptional person, and I'd like you to meet her." That was definitely new for him. She had met Alana a few times, but it had never been important to him, and he had discouraged it. Alana wasn't interested in his family anyway. Wendy wondered if Violet was any different or just another opportunist, which came with the territory. Andy attracted them like moths to flame, though probably less so now without a studio and an important job behind him. But he was making a movie anyway, so that might be enough to attract other ambitious women. Wendy worried about him falling hard for one of them, but so far he never had. This one might be different. She was concerned and had spoken to her husband about it. Peter said that there was enough to worry about with Wendy's dad right now, and the blow to his ego and concern about his future, that there was no need to add worries about a woman to the mix. Peter was sure that Andy was in no mood for romance. He had enough on his plate without that and was feeling the pain of the blow to his image and stature in Hollywood. It could be a very cruel place, and Andy had felt the sharp end of it, as Peter knew. He had extended his sympathy to his father-in-law when he got fired, and Andy had sounded terrible, like a broken man, in the first few days afterward. Peter had never heard him like that before, and had been genuinely concerned.

* * *

They had almost finished filming the movie when Andy left alone to spend Thanksgiving in New York with Wendy, her husband, and their children. Violet was working on the set and writing furiously at night. Andy was thrilled to see his family, and stayed in Greenwich with them. Wendy was happy to be with him too, and thought he was in better emotional shape and spirits than she'd seen in years. He seemed peaceful and happy, and was excited about the movie he was working on, which was a small one, but he said it was a gem. He spoke respectfully and lovingly of Violet, which made Wendy more curious than ever about her. And she had never seen her father so peaceful and calm. He seemed genuinely happy.

He enjoyed his grandchildren too, although his daughter was the main event for him. She was loved in her job and her marriage. They had a lovely home, and a wide circle of friends. He remembered those years when he was the same age as Wendy and Peter. He was still screenwriting then, before he became head of Global Studios, and he hadn't started neglecting his family yet. Most of the damage had been done later. But when she was small, as Wendy's children were now, he had enjoyed her, and he and Jean had been happier than they were later on, once their marriage had disintegrated from neglect on his part. He always readily accepted his responsibility for the divorce.

He enjoyed the holiday with the family, carved the turkey, and flew back to London on Sunday. Violet was waiting for him when he got back to the apartment in Notting Hill. Dash had texted him that they had rushed through the weekend and were ready to wrap the film. He had arranged for a special preview showing of the film in order to qualify for the Golden Globes.

"How was it?" Violet asked him when she put her arms around him and kissed him. He had texted her all weekend but hadn't called, nor had she, not wanting to intrude.

"Like a Norman Rockwell painting. A big golden turkey, a table full of food, two beautiful children, a happy young couple, the crystal and silver gleaming. It was perfect. I'm glad I went. She's a happy young woman with a nice husband, sweet kids, and a good job. I couldn't want anything more for her." Violet was only six years older than Wendy, but she had been through so much that she seemed more mature. Wendy had lived a golden, easy life, except for her father's absence for much of it. But her own marriage seemed warm and solid. She had chosen well. And Peter came from a good family of two sisters, a brother, and loving parents who had set their children a good example of a solid marriage, not like him and Jean.

"What's new here?" he asked Violet.

"The bank notified me that the house finally sold in the auction. It went for almost nothing. Gabe spent a fortune on it. But I'm glad it's gone." They hadn't gotten back there for a weekend after they left, as Andy had suspected they wouldn't, so they didn't need to go back for anything. It had served them well for a few months, but given its history for Violet, he was relieved for her that it was out of her life at last and she'd never have to see it again. A page had turned. "The woman at the bank said a Saudi couple with five children bought it, and they were very happy. They're going to use it as a summer home." Violet smiled happily at him. "And I've been working on the new movie all week-end. I can't wait for you to read what I've got." It was too late for him to read it that night. He was tired, but she was so obviously excited about it that he was eager to read it too. She was already think-ing ahead to the next chapter of their lives.

They were going straight into postproduction, and were ready for it, so they could release the film before Christmas. Everyone was going to be work-ing round the clock on postproduction. The unions would never have allowed that on a studio film. But the independents could do whatever they wanted if their employees were willing, and paid enough overtime. Both Dash and Andy were happy to foot the bill for that. They wanted to get the film out in time to be considered for the Golden Globe Awards in January and the Academy Awards in March. If they won anything at all, it would make the film a much bigger commercial success and establish Andy's reputation as a screenwriter and Violet's for the original story she'd written. It could be the start of a big career for her, and a dream come true.

The last day of shooting was very emotional for the cast, and everyone who worked on the picture. The final scenes were beautifully filmed and deeply moving and every one of the performers gave it their best, with Henry's meticulous direction. He was an extraordinary director. Andy even cried when he watched them film the last scene, and Dash had tears in his eyes too. There were hugs and tears and tender goodbyes, as they all left the set that had been home to them for three months.

Postproduction was scheduled to start at six A.M. the next day, and Dash was going to be there. Andy had promised to come in too. And Violet was going with him, to learn more about the process. He'd had time to read her new material by then, and he loved it. It was about a close family on a farm in the Midwest and what happens to each of them once they grow up. Violet was fascinated with down-to-earth American values. They symbolized the best of family life to her, rather than more formal, distant British rules. It was a strong, emotional piece. With the right actors, Andy could see it becoming a big hit in the States. It showed a whole other side of

Violet's talent as a writer. He had already talked to Dash about it, and depending on how their first movie performed in the next few weeks, he was willing to do another film with them. Violet still had to write it, but she had a strong outline and all the infrastructure in place. She had learned a lot on their first film.

With everyone working around the clock, they had the special preview, made the list for the Golden Globe nominations for Best Dramatic Picture just in time, and got the movie into the theaters with their distribution deal. By the week after Christmas, they knew they had a hit on their hands. The numbers were unbelievable. It was the thriller of the season. Everybody wanted to see it. The critics loved it and so did the audiences. Dash and Andy were going to make their money back and a healthy profit, Violet was on her way for the original story, and Andy's script got rave reviews.

"I told you that you should be making indie movies," Dash reminded him. Violet and Andy went out to dinner with Dash to celebrate. Andy called every member of the cast and crew to thank them for their hard work. And Violet and Andy spent a quiet Christmas together. He took her to Paris for New Year's Eve, and they stayed at the Ritz. He loved spoiling her, because she never expected it, and was so touched whenever he did. She was the easiest, most undemanding, caring woman he'd ever known.

As soon as they got back from Paris the day after New Year's, Violet went back to working on her new movie every day. Andy read what she'd written at the end of the day, and loved the way she was developing it. There were going to be rich roles for a star-studded cast. The characters were poignant and touching, the story deeply moving. She had a real gift. She had already moved on emotionally from the movie they had just finished and was in love with her new story, while Andy read box office reports on their current movie in the States. It was breaking records.

The Golden Globes awards ceremony was scheduled a week later than usual, in two weeks, and Violet, Andy, and Dash were supposed to fly to LA together and were planning to stay at Andy's house in Bel Air. Andy was feeling anxious about the trip and his return to LA. He had suggested that Dash and Violet go without him, and they insisted he had to go, in case they won Best Dramatic Picture, which Andy thought unlikely. He argued vehemently not to go.

"You don't need me there," he had said to Dash.

"Are you crazy? We're nominated for Best Dramatic Picture. Of course you have to go."

"You and Violet can accept it for me. And it's a long shot that we'll win anyway, for a little indie picture."

"Andy, you've got to go." Dash was insistent, though Violet understood how hard it was for him.

"For God's sake, I got fired nine months ago. I was the head of a studio. And now I turn up as screenwriter on an indie film? I'll look ridiculous. I'll get laughed out of the theater. You don't know what the movie world is like. And if we don't win, I'll look like a fool. I'm not going," he said stubbornly to Violet, as she gently tried to convince him, and at first he wouldn't budge. But she was as determined as he was, and knew how scared he was to face his old world in LA. He felt like a ghost from the past.

She heard him arguing heatedly with Dash about it. She could see how upset he was. He was flushed and crossed the room to pour himself a drink at their makeshift bar. "You don't need that," she said gently to him, after he ended the conversation with Dash.

"Yes, I do. Dash is pushing me to go to LA. I'd make a fool of myself if I go. From studio head to screenwriter. 'How far the mighty have fallen.' I will **not** go. He wants me at the awards ceremony. You do too, of course. And I don't want to let you down, but you don't need me there. I'll stay here and start working on the screenplay for the next picture that you're already working on."

"It's been almost a year," she said gently, "and you wrote the script for a brilliant movie. Your screenplay is fantastic. Our movie deserves to win, and even if it doesn't, you have to go back to LA someday. And the awards ceremony is the perfect reason."

"If we win, I'll look foolish, and if we lose, I'll look even worse."

"This isn't about you," Violet reminded him. "It's about all of us who worked on it. Our picture is fantastic, and so is your screenplay."

"I'll look like I did it out of desperation, just to get a job."

"You did it because you're a talented writer. That's why you're nominated. You've got to go back. What better way to do it than this, nominated for a prestigious award?" Andy growled at her and set his drink down.

"Vi, I can't." He looked desperate, and grief-stricken again.

"Yes, you can, and I'll be with you." He sat staring into space for a minute, thinking about it. He really didn't want to go. It would be humiliating, in front of all the people who had looked up to him before, who had envied him, and wanted to be him. Now he was just a writer, a failure. He'd been fired. The agony of the humiliation he had suffered seemed as vivid as it had the day he got fired.

He finished his drink and followed Violet to bed, and had nightmares about it that night. People laughed him off the stage when he won the award. He looked terrible at breakfast. Dash called half an hour later. They were supposed to leave for LA the next day.

"I haven't changed my mind," Andy said stubbornly.

"Neither have I," Dash said just as firmly. He called Violet on her cellphone half an hour later.

"Vi, you have to make him go."

"I can't carry him onto the plane. He thinks it will be humiliating. He hasn't been to LA in nine months."

"He can't hide forever. He has to face them all sooner or later."

"He thinks he's not ready."

"The longer he waits, the worse it'll get. Talk to him. You're the only one who can make him do it."

"I'll try, but I don't think he'll go." She thought he should, but she respected his right not to.

She talked to him about it that afternoon and he was nearly in tears over it. "Vi, it was the worst thing that ever happened in my career. I can't face all those people now."

"You're being nominated for an award. That's a huge honor. You can't just turn away from that. We can leave the day after. You don't have to stick around. But I think you should face it and get it over with. You need to show yourself you can do it, more than anyone else. It won't be as bad as you think. And I'll be there with you every minute."

He looked at her with a slow smile. She was so patient and kind to him, and she was always so brave. He didn't want to look like a coward to her. He touched her cheek and then he kissed her.

"I'll do it for you," he said softly. "But I'm leaving as soon as it's over, maybe even that night."

"That's all you have to do, in and out, and then you don't ever have to be afraid to go back again. Besides, I want to see your house." He smiled.

"It's a cool house. I'd love to be there with you if it weren't in LA."

He followed her into the bedroom then and took out his suitcase. He pulled his tuxedo out of the closet. He had brought it to England, but hadn't worn it since the last Academy Awards, right before he got fired. She packed for him, while she tried to figure out what to wear. She didn't have time to buy a gown. She pulled out the only long black dress she still owned. She had saved it but never worn it. It wasn't exciting, but it would do. She finished packing, put her suitcase in the hall next to his, and then got into bed and held him. He looked upset and she gently stroked his face until he fell asleep. She hoped everything would go well in LA. She didn't want him to get hurt again. He didn't deserve it. And his resistance to going told them both that the wound was still deep and hadn't healed. Maybe it never would.

Chapter 14

The flight to LA took off from Heathrow at ten o'clock the next morning. The three of them were traveling first class, at the producers' expense, Dash and Andy. The stars, Marilyn Gray and Godfrey Hunt, were meeting them there and had gone ahead a few days before. They were going to stay at Andy's house too. Andy was quiet when they got on the plane. Violet took her seat next to him. She had texted Timothy, the butler at Andy's LA house, that morning, to tell him five of them would be arriving. Andy had sent Wendy an email to tell her he was going and invited her to come. There would be a dinner before the ceremony, and as nominees, they were given a table. Violet had seen it on TV, but never been there. This was a big deal for her and for all of them. She was proud of their movie, and proud of Andy for deciding to

go. She knew better than anyone how hard it was
for him.

Andy slept for the first half of the flight. Violet
didn't disturb him and covered him with a blanket.
Then he woke up and had lunch, and after that
he watched a movie. He didn't talk to Violet and
Dash. He was viscerally upset about going back to
LA. He felt sick whenever he thought about it.

It was a long flight, eleven hours, and an hour
before they landed, Andy sat staring out the window, lost in thought. Then he turned and smiled
at Violet.

"I'm sorry I've been such a pain in the ass about
going. It's humiliating to go back. It's like reliving what happened a year ago." He had never
faced it then. He had hidden in his house for two
weeks and then fled to England. Now he had to
go back and face them all, all the jealous and the
naysayers, and people who had predicted his career was over and that he'd never get a comparable
job, and he was too old. He had proven some of
them wrong and written an outstanding screenplay,
which showed that he had talent. But he wasn't returning in victory. He wasn't back as the head of a
studio. He had made an indie movie, which wasn't
nearly the same thing. He wasn't back on top, and
he was sure he never would be again. Those jobs
just didn't open up very often, and nothing had
changed in the past year. The heads of studios didn't

give up their jobs unless they were terminally sick, died, or got fired.

When the plane landed, Andy looked tense. They were met at the door of the plane by the airline's VIP team and escorted through customs rapidly. Violet had been to LA with Gabe, and to New York, but it was different coming with Andy. LA was his previous kingdom. Now he was only a deposed king. He was no one, which was how he felt.

The butler had hired a driver to pick them up at the airport, since Andy no longer had one. The last one had been provided by the studio. The driver had come to the airport in Andy's Bentley. All along the way in the airport, airline staff had greeted him and welcomed him back to the States. The customs officials had done the same, and a Homeland Security officer shook Andy's hand. Watching how they addressed him, and the natural grace with which Andy handled it, began to show Violet just how important he had been, and still was. He was like a visiting dignitary or an ex-president. He hadn't been forgotten by any means. Far from it.

"Maybe no one told them I got fired," Andy whispered to her as they got into his car.

"Maybe they still think you're important, because you are," she whispered back, and Andy didn't answer. He hadn't known what to expect on arrival. But he had also previously had one of the largest private planes at LAX waiting on call for him at all times. People didn't forget that. Some of them had been surprised he was flying commercial now.

It took them an hour to get through LA traffic and get to the house. Marilyn and Godfrey were already there, waiting for them to arrive. What staff he had left were lined up in the driveway to greet him. They could see the pool as they entered the house, and Dash whistled, as Marilyn and Godfrey came to greet them.

"Not bad, Andy," Dash said, and Andy smiled, as Timothy, the butler, gave Andy a warm welcome. A light meal had been set out for them in the dining room, and the maids bustled around and took the luggage to the rooms they'd been assigned. Timothy informed Marilyn and Violet that hairdressers, makeup artists, and manicurists had been arranged for them before the awards dinner the following night.

"You run a very smooth, elegant operation here," Dash complimented Andy. Dash was wearing a wrinkled suit, the only one he had, a T-shirt and sneakers, and his hair was a wild mane of dark tangled curls. He hadn't shaved in five days. Andy was used to the way Dash looked, and he looked no worse than anyone else in Hollywood these days. Godfrey Hunt looked impeccable and like a movie star in a blazer and white jeans and alligator loafers. Marilyn looked glamorous in white pants and a pink sweater with an Hermès bag. She got to keep her costumes on most pictures. Violet had traveled in jeans and a black leather jacket, with her dark hair pulled back.

"I didn't know your house would be this grand," she whispered to Andy, looking embarrassed, as she ate one of the impeccably trimmed sandwiches that had been left for them on silver trays. "I don't have anything fancy to wear." She was beginning to wonder if he was going to be embarrassed going to the awards with her in her plain black dress. Marilyn had borrowed a dress from Dior in London. Dash had bought a tuxedo off the rack at Saint Laurent the day before. Godfrey had his own, made to order for him in Rome, and Andy's was from his London tailor, who made all his clothes.

The others wandered around the ground floor, admiring the art, and Godfrey stopped in front of Andy's parents' movie posters. "I love his movies," he said reverently. "I'm a huge fan. You too?" he said, and Andy smiled. He loved seeing the familiar posters again. He had missed them.

"He was my father," Andy said simply. Godfrey hadn't made the connection with the same last name and felt foolish, as he stared at Andy.

"Oh my God. He was one of the all-time greats. I've seen all his movies."

"Me too," Dash said. He already knew about Andy's father. Violet looked at them carefully too, realizing not only that Andy had had an important job, but that he was a member of Hollywood royalty, and no one could take that away from him. Being in LA with him gave her a glimpse of what his life had been like before he left. He exuded power and was an important man here. In England he was able to get lost in the crowd now if he tried hard enough. In LA, there was no way he could. She understood now why he hadn't wanted to come, but she was glad he had. He needed to be reminded that this was who he was, and had been long before he was the head of Global Studios.

They all went to their rooms and Timothy told them that dinner would be served at eight o'clock, and they were welcome to swim before that. They had opted to stay home that night, and dinner had been ordered from Andy's favorite Mexican restaurant.

When he got to his room with Violet, she looked around his enormous bedroom, at the antiques and the art, the framed mementos, and sat down on the bed. It was late for them with the time difference.

"Your house makes my old house look like a shack," she said, and he laughed. "Did your daughter grow up in this house?"

"No. I gave her mother the house she grew up in. I bought this one after the divorce. It's my bachelor pad. I used to entertain a lot here, before I got too busy."

"It's an incredible place. Are you sure you wouldn't rather go to the ceremony with some movie star? You can always say that Marilyn is your date, and

I'll just go with Dash." She meant it, and he could see how shy she felt. She didn't feel equal to his lifestyle. She didn't have the clothes for it and didn't want to embarrass him.

"As my mother used to say, Dash looks like an unmade bed. You're here with me, and I'm proud to be going to the awards ceremony with you. I'll walk the red carpet with you, Vi, not some movie star. You're my star." He had grown up in the spotlight and it was second nature to him. Being a studio head was part of it, but his own history and who he was were a bigger part, she saw now. When he ran away to England after he was fired, he forgot who he had been before Global Studios came into his life. No one could take any of that away from him. He was a star in his own right, without being a studio head. She reminded him of it while they showered and dressed for dinner.

"I forget that sometimes," he said, as he thought about it. "I like being in Europe because I can disappear. I can't disappear here."

"You don't need to. You can be you, whether you're head of a studio, or writing a screenplay for a movie. You get to do whatever you want to do. People are always going to be jealous of you, because of who you are and who your parents were, how you live and what you drive. You don't need to hide anymore, Andy. You can be whoever you want and do what you want," she said gently, as he buttoned an immaculate white shirt, and put on jeans and brown suede shoes, and she put on jeans and a red sweater with red flats.

He was happy she was there, and it felt good to be home. He had forgotten how much he liked his house. He had been gone for so long. They walked down the stairs from his bedroom holding hands, and out onto the patio where the others were waiting and drinking margaritas Timothy had made. They were delicious, everyone agreed. Dash was swimming, but the others were dressed. Dash reminded Andy of a big friendly Labrador who would shake his mop of wet hair and get them all wet. He and Violet helped themselves to margaritas and sat down with the others. There was heat coming from the floor of the patio and it was comfortable sitting outside.

"If I had this house, I would never leave LA," Dash said, as he toweled off after his swim. Timothy appeared, handed him a terry-cloth robe, and Dash helped himself to one of the margaritas and looked blissfully happy in a lounge chair.

Andy had gotten an email from Wendy when he landed that both her children and their nanny were sick, and she wouldn't be able to come to LA, but she'd be watching the awards on TV.

"I guess turnabout is fair play," he said quietly to Violet when he got the email. "I never went to any of her awards ceremonies either. Her mother did. I was always working. I don't think we'll win anyway." But he wanted Violet and Wendy to meet one of these days. He and Violet would have to go to New York.

Dash went upstairs to change after he finished his drink, and came back in cutoff jeans, and a short while later, they helped themselves to the Mexican buffet in the dining room and sat down at a beautifully set table with a long centerpiece of red flowers. They were all impressed by how graciously Andy lived. He realized too how strange it was to be there without Frances helping him, but Timothy was managing well without her. She was still enjoying her new job, and she was in Aspen for the winter with her new boss. Her mother was in a care facility in Palm Springs now, but doing well. Frances stayed in touch with Andy.

Godfrey asked Andy during dinner how many people he had working at the house, and Andy looked blank for a minute and laughed.

"I don't know. I've been gone for almost a year." And they had all been there waiting for him to come back.

"Now I know how rich and important you are, if you don't even know how many employees you have. I have a cleaning woman twice a week."

"I probably have too many," Andy admitted. "I'm very spoiled."

"You certainly are," Dash agreed with him, and they all laughed, even Andy. "I want to be you when I grow up, if I ever do."

Andy was happy to see Violet relax as the evening wore on. The house was beautiful and impressive, full of valuable art and objects, but he was still the same man she lived with in London and was in love with, in the rented apartment in Notting Hill, with the battered furniture. There was nothing arrogant or pretentious about him. He just lived very well, and he could afford to. But he was just as comfortable living simply with Violet. It was nice to be able to do both.

They all went to bed early that night, after the long flight, and came down to breakfast in the morning. Andy looked happy now that he was there, with his friends around him, in his luxurious home, but as the day wore on, they could all feel the tension mount, and Andy looked stressed when they got into the cars at five o'clock to do the red carpet at the Hilton Hotel where the awards dinner and ceremony were being held. Andy was dreading it, and the rude questions the press would inevitably ask, and the comments people would make to cut him down to size and remind him he'd been fired. He looked deeply unhappy as Violet got in beside him in the Bentley driven by a driver hired for the night. Another hired driver drove the others in the Range Rover. Violet was wearing her simple black dress. She looked beautiful in it, the makeup artist had done her face lightly with just a little eye makeup and blush. She had her own natural beauty, and the hairdresser had combed out her shining dark hair and left it down.

"You look gorgeous," he whispered to her. Marilyn was wearing a slinky silver dress, and the men were in tuxedos. And as soon as they got to the red carpet at the Hilton, the press started shouting Marilyn's and Godfrey's names, and another group of them broke away and called Andy's name and begged him and Violet to pose for pictures. Andy looked elegant and dignified and as handsome as ever. Nothing had changed in the last year, except his job. He was still who he was.

"Welcome back!" several of them called out to him, and Violet stood next to him, looking beautiful and natural. "You've been making indie pictures!" one of them shouted. "And you're up for an award for **Tightrope.** Your dad would be proud. Like your dad directing. Are you going to produce more indies?" one reporter called out to him.

"I hope so!" Andy called back and smiled at Violet. His homecoming to LA had gone smoother than he had expected. No one had mentioned Global Studios, or the fact that he'd been fired. It was as though they had forgotten, and they were interested in his new career now as the producer of indie pictures. Just like his father's transition from actor to director. He realized, as the group made their way to their table after the red carpet, that he had come home, and he was still a hero in his hometown. He felt a wave of relief wash over him as he leaned over and kissed Violet. She was beaming at him, proud to be with him, as he was to be with her.

He saw Alana in the distance a little while later, with the same studio head he and Violet had seen her with in Portofino. He looked even older in his tuxedo, and Alana was glancing around the room for important people to talk to. She seemed not to see Andy, and he had the feeling that she had and was embarrassed to say hello to him in public, not sure which way the wind was blowing for him.

Their group had a good time at dinner, and the awards ceremony was exciting once it started. All of the nominees were nervous as they waited interminably for their category to come up. It was a long wait as the other categories were announced and the trophies handed out. He and Dash exchanged a look as the Best Dramatic Picture nominees were announced at last. The presenter ran through the nominees, and Andy heard Violet give a gasp, and Dash half rose from his chair and looked at Andy. "We won!" Marilyn shouted, and Dash and Andy went up on the stage to accept the awards, each of them said a few words, briefly, and then they were back at the table, looking stunned. Dash held his globe high in the air, and Andy set his down in front of Violet and she kissed him.

"Congratulations!" she said, and he smiled at her. She'd been right all along. He was glad he'd come, and he had a feeling his father would have been proud too.

"Thank you for the great story," he said to Violet, as everyone at the table congratulated him.

It was a perfect evening. They went to one of the after-parties, and then went back to Andy's house and drank champagne by the pool, and Violet gave a start when she heard her phone vibrate and she looked at the message, and then at Andy.

"That's weird. I have a message from a woman I don't know at Webber Communications. Helen Berg. She wants me to call her. What's that about? Do you know her?"

"She's the head of TV. She's a big deal there. You should call her in the morning," Andy told her. Violet couldn't imagine why the woman had called her. They sat together and drank champagne for another hour, and then Andy and Violet went up to bed, and he set his trophy down on the dresser and looked at it with a broad grin, finally beginning to feel comfortable with having won.

"That looks pretty good, doesn't it?" He was surprised at how good it felt to win. And then he smiled at her. "You'll win next time," he said to her. "Thank you for making me come home." He was comfortable in LA again. The demons had been laid to rest. He was no longer the studio head who had been fired. He was the award-winning producer of independent movies now. The tides had turned while he was away, starting a new life.

Chapter 15

The morning after the Golden Globe Awards, at Andy's urging, Violet called Helen Berg at Webber Communications. She had no idea what the woman wanted or how she had gotten her name, but Andy insisted that she was important, and she might be an interesting contact to have. Webber was a streaming service that also placed major original shows on TV, and according to Andy, Helen Berg was the head of TV.

When Violet called the number Berg had left, it was obvious that she was expecting Violet's call when the assistant who had answered said, "I'll put you right through." Helen Berg came on the line immediately and sounded very pleased.

"First, let me congratulate you on your Golden Globe win last night for Best Picture. I saw it, and it's a spectacular film. You had me on the edge of my seat for the entire movie, and I don't say that very often."

"Thank you. We had a terrific cast and director, and a wonderful screenplay."

"I had no idea that Andy Westfield had started his career as a screenwriter. He has a real gift. I hope we'll see more of his work soon," Berg said.

"I hope so too," Violet said. "We're starting a new project now."

"Before you get too deep into it, I'd love to toss some ideas around with you. It could be to our mutual benefit. Did you write any of the script yourself?"

"I tried my hand at a few scenes. I'm learning from Andy, but I don't have his talent or experience."

"I'm sure you have the talent, and the experience will come with time. He must be a great teacher."

"He is."

"I know you're here from England for a short visit," Helen Berg said pleasantly. At Andy's insistence, Violet had an agent now. Helen Berg had researched it and called him for Violet's contact information, and he had told her she was only staying for two days. "I'd love to spend a few minutes with you before you go back. I'm sorry I called you so late last night. I wanted to catch you before you leave. You must have been celebrating. I'm sure you know that the Academy often follows the Golden Globes pretty closely. How long will you be here?" Andy was planning to change their tickets that day. He originally wanted to leave the morning after the awards, but since the trip had gone well so far, he had agreed to stay a few more days.

"I'm not sure. We were planning to leave today, but we all want to stay a little longer. We love LA."

"Do you live in London?" Helen was curious about Violet.

"I just moved back. I've been living in a sleepy little beach town for the last eleven years. Our producer's studios are right outside London. I'm going to stay in London now. It's great to be back."

"Would you have time to come to see me today?" Violet knew no more about why Helen wanted to speak to her than she had before she returned her call. "I won't take up too much of your time, but I have some ideas that might be of interest to you. I'd love to meet you. Would sometime this afternoon work for you?" Violet didn't know what Andy's plans were for the day, but she knew he wanted to see his attorney and his financial advisor at some point, instead of constantly dealing with them by email and on the phone. "How does four o'clock fit in with your plans?"

"I can make it work," Violet answered. "I'm very curious about what you have in mind," she said to Helen.

"Let's talk about it when we meet," Helen said easily. She gave Violet the address, and after the call Violet went to find Andy. He was getting dressed in his dressing room.

"I still have no idea why she called. She wants to 'toss some ideas around' with me. What does that mean?"

"I don't know either, but she's a smart woman and a big deal at Webber. You should definitely go talk to her," Andy encouraged her.

"She loved our movie." Violet smiled at him.

"We're going to get a lot of calls like hers. A lot of them will be bullshit, or people looking for work from us. But Helen Berg is definitely worth seeing."

"Do you want to come?" she asked him hopefully, and he smiled at her.

"She asked to see you, not me. She won't eat you. Go and see her," he encouraged her again.

"She wanted me to come at four."

"That's perfect. I've got boring appointments this afternoon. I was going to tell you to go shopping if you want."

"I'll do that before I see her," Violet said, and went to get dressed herself. She was sharing his spacious dressing room with him. He had an extra bathroom and walk-in closet for female guests, but not large enough for anyone to want to move in. He'd been clever about that with his architect and decorator. Violet had brought very little with her, since they were originally only going to stay for two days. She owned very few clothes anyway, everything she had of value had been seized by the prosecutor when Gabriel got arrested. She didn't miss having a big wardrobe and the jewelry he had bought her, she knew they were all bought at the expense of other people. She never went anywhere for all the years afterward. Now she needed some new clothes for their life in London, and she could afford to pay for them herself. Andy had offered to buy things for her, but she didn't want to take advantage of him. Andy and Dash had paid her handsomely for the story.

Violet had brought a plain navy blue pantsuit to travel in on the trip back and decided to wear that to the meeting. One of the maids took it to press it for her, and she had a pair of black high heels with her to wear with it, and a pair of gold earrings. The weather in LA was mild compared to London.

With only slight trepidation compared to what he'd felt before they came, Andy made a lunch reservation for them at the Polo Lounge at the Beverly Hills Hotel, and he explained to Violet what an important meeting place it was for everyone in the film industry. He drove her to lunch himself in his Bentley sports car, and had Timothy follow them in the other Bentley, a sedan, so Timothy could drive her after lunch when Andy left her for his meetings.

When Andy and Violet walked into the Polo Lounge, heads turned. He nodded to a few people but didn't stop to talk to anyone. He had asked for a quiet table. It was a little too chilly to eat in the garden, which he usually preferred. The maître d' and all the waiters knew him. And the only word Andy and Violet had heard so far all day was "Congratulations," and at the Polo Lounge, "Good to see you back, Mr. Westfield. . . . Wonderful to see you. . . . We've missed you." Several people stopped at their table after lunch and seemed genuinely happy to see Andy. He was relieved to see that he had stayed away long enough that people seemed to have lost interest in his sudden career change ten months before. It was old news now, and his prize-winning indie film was a much bigger and more interesting subject. He had come back as a winner after all, more than he had realized. And the Golden Globe Award had won him new respect.

The number of people who came by, their obvious admiration, and the diligent attention of all the employees illustrated to Violet again how large a figure Andy was on the LA scene. She realized just how important he was, and what it meant that he had taken her under his wing and gotten her manuscript turned into a movie. He was a **very** big deal in LA. She could also see now all he had given up when he came to England, all the comforts and luxuries and his beautiful house in Bel-Air.

"You must miss it," she said to him gently over lunch. He had recommended the McCarthy salad to her, and she loved it.

"I do miss it sometimes, it's comfortable and

familiar," he admitted, "but there were other advantages to being in England for the past year, like meeting you for instance." He smiled at her.

"Maybe we could come back and visit sometimes," she said cautiously, not wanting to push him.

"We're going to be busy with your new movie for the coming months." He wasn't rushing back to LA yet, but he was obviously enjoying being there, and he looked much more relaxed than when they arrived. And he seemed more at ease and confident.

When they left the restaurant, Andy looked genuinely happy. No one had made any unpleasant comments, and a paparazzo took a photograph of him and Violet and smiled at them both. Andy reclaimed his car and left for his meetings, and Violet went with Timothy in the other Bentley to discover the wonders of Rodeo Drive. She half expected to see Marilyn there, but she didn't. The others were out doing their own thing. Godfrey had friends in town, Marilyn was shopping, and Dash had set up some meetings with agents.

At three-thirty, Violet left to go to her meeting. It was in a skyscraper downtown, and she followed Helen Berg's directions closely once she got there so she wouldn't get lost in a cluster of similar buildings.

The Webber Communications offices were on the thirtieth floor, and when Violet checked in at the desk an assistant came out to get her immediately, and she was whisked away to Helen Berg's office, which had a sweeping view of the city, and a seating area. Helen Berg stood up to greet Violet warmly as soon as she walked into the room. When it was offered, Violet asked for tea and they sat in big comfortable beige leather chairs around a low table. Helen Berg was a stylishly dressed slim woman somewhere in her late forties with well-cut short gray hair and was the only woman Violet had seen so far who didn't look like she'd had a face-lift. She looked like a real person. She was businesslike as she finally revealed the mysterious reason for asking Violet to come and see her.

"We're working on a number of new dramatic series, and since you wrote the original story that the movie was based on, I was wondering if you'd be interested in writing the bible for one of our new series, something in the vein of your movie. A thriller with a female star. We'd like it if you would write the screenplay too, but we can find someone to do it if you don't want to. The only hitch is that we're working on next season, so we'd have to get on it very quickly." It was an invitation which any writer in Hollywood would have given their right arm for, but when Violet heard the timing, she knew she couldn't do it. She didn't want to miss the opportunity of working on another movie with Andy.

"It sounds like an incredible opportunity," Violet said honestly, "but I've already started a new project with the same producers. But I'd be very interested in something like that in the future, and by then, maybe I'd feel ready to tackle the script. I don't think I'm ready to do that yet. My original story was in book form. Andy Westfield wrote the screenplay for **Tightrope** based on my manuscript."

"That's what I understood, which is why I called you. We would love to have you in our Webber stable of very talented writers. Are you and Andy writing partners? Should we be talking to him too? I had the impression that the picture was kind of a one-off for him. I assumed he'd want to wind up running another studio one of these days. Do you think he'd be interested in working on a series with you? He could certainly write the scripts if you're more comfortable working with him," Helen said easily, eager to please and to entice Violet to sign on with them.

"I'm not sure what his long-term plans are. I think he wants to pick and choose his writing projects. I loved working with him. And he taught me a lot about the process."

"With spectacular results, I might add." Helen smiled at Violet. "I'm sorry you're not free right now, Violet. We would have loved to have you on our lead series for the fall, with all the hype that goes with it. We could schedule it for later in the season, but a new show has more impact if we launch it in the fall. We can always consider it for January or February. Or wait till the year after.

We're very interested in partnering with you, and that's by unanimous vote of the committee that green-lights our new projects."

"I'm really honored," Violet said, her head swimming with all the information Helen had given her. She wanted to remember every detail to tell Andy when she got home.

They chatted for a few more minutes. Helen thanked her for her time, and Violet thanked her for the very flattering opportunity.

"Don't just be flattered. Come and work for us," Helen said, smiling. "I'm sure you'll get a lot of offers, but we would really love to put a show of yours on the air, as soon as you feel you could do it, with your other commitments."

"I'd love that too, and I'll talk to Andy about it. I think he's still a little torn right now between another big executive job and writing."

"I know which one I'd pick," Helen said. "I'd pick writing. It's fresh every day, and you have a lot more control of your own destiny and can pretty much establish your conditions. My idea of hell would be running a studio or a network. He's remarkable that he managed to hang in at Global for nineteen years. Most people burn out in two. It's a thankless high-risk job, and if the owners sell, you're out of a job, just like Andy. It happens all the time in this business. It's brutal dealing with that kind of insecurity, one minute you're at the top, and the next minute you're on the street, looking for a new job. Some of the best people I know have lost their jobs that way, when the parent company sells. I think Andy handled it with enormous grace. He was smart to leave town for a while and do something else. Give him my best. We worked on a project together years ago, he probably doesn't even remember me," Helen said modestly.

"Oh yes, he does. Very much so. He wanted me to come to this meeting, and spoke highly of you."

"Good. I'm happy to hear it. Next time, he's welcome to join us." Helen walked Violet back to the reception area on her floor, and Violet was elated when she got in the elevator. She couldn't wait to talk to Andy about it. She had liked Helen Berg a lot. She seemed like a supremely competent woman and a straight shooter.

Timothy drove Violet to a few more shops on the way home. She was distracted, thinking about everything Helen Berg had said to her, and she was waiting impatiently for Andy with a glass of wine at the pool when he got back to the house at six o'clock. He stopped to kiss her and sat down in a chair next to her. "How was your meeting?" he asked her. He was happy to see her when he got home.

"I think it was pretty good." She repeated everything Helen said to her.

"Pretty good? Vi, it was fantastic! People here

would die for an offer like that from Webber. And you turned it down? I can't believe it."

"I want to work on our new movie with you," she said simply. "I can always talk to her after that."

"If they're still interested. Things move fast in this business. You shouldn't miss an opportunity like that."

"I'd rather work with you on another movie," she said, and he smiled at her.

"I don't know how I got so lucky. This town is crawling with people who would kill their grandmothers to get an opportunity like that, and you just turned down your own series at Webber. She must have been surprised."

"Maybe. She said you could do the scripts on the new show if we want to continue working together. She asked if we're writing partners. I wasn't sure what to say."

"Yes, we are. I have to admit, a big series would be kind of a thrill, and we could probably squeeze in an indie movie once a year. Now, that would be a great combo." She smiled then too.

"It sounded good to me, but I wanted to hear what you thought."

"I think you were crazy to turn it down, but hopefully you'll get another shot. And I know I love you. That's what I think of your meeting. If you want to keep writing together, I think what she's suggesting could even be good for us. Thank you for holding out for our movie," he said gratefully.

"There was no way I was going to give that up," she said, as Dash arrived at the house and came to talk to them at the pool.

"I want to move to LA," he said, looking excited. "I love the weather here, the food, and the people."

Andy turned to him with a grin. "Violet turned down the offer of a series for Webber today," he said proudly, and Dash's eyes opened wide.

"You're shitting me."

"I'm not. She didn't want to miss the chance to work on another movie with us."

"Hell, I would have sold your ass out in a hot minute," Dash said, and all three of them laughed. "And I mean it. What was the series about?"

"Whatever Violet wants to write. Carte blanche," Andy said.

Dash groaned. "I'm dying." And then he turned to her. "Next time you get an offer like that, call me before you decline. We need to protect you."

Dash chatted with them for a little while, and then went out to meet friends for dinner.

The rest of their visit to LA went smoothly. Andy took Violet to some of his favorite haunts, shops, and restaurants, even an old-fashioned diner. They swam in his pool, and at the end of four days, the whole group went back to London, where they were met by grisly cold weather. They all missed LA. It had been a wonderful trip, and Andy had brought back his Golden Globe and set it on the mantelpiece of the living room in the Notting

Hill apartment, which seemed tiny and even less charming now that Andy and Violet had been in his beautiful, spacious home in Bel-Air. Andy commented once they were back that they needed to find a better apartment if they were going to spend another six months in London, working on their new movie. The Notting Hill apartment hadn't been meant to be long-term, and it seemed crowded now.

Violet understood him better now that she had seen his LA home, and had observed him in his natural habitat, how well he lived, how important he was even now, without being a studio head. It was a lot to give up and to run away from, into the anonymity he had embraced in England. He would always be an object of admiration and envy in LA. He couldn't escape it. But he had given up so many good things along with the bad. They talked about the Webber offer again, but he was less interested in a series than she was. He preferred making movies to television. He was more familiar with the medium, and touched that she had turned the opportunity down to work with him.

They dove into the new movie as soon as they got back, and he taught her more about how to construct a screenplay this time, and she wrote several scenes herself to blend with his. They were in total agreement about what to preserve from her material and what was crucial to the essence of the story. She had a great strength for character development, and he had an unfailing instinct about the flow of the story to hold the viewers' interest. Their talents blended in perfect harmony, and the second movie seemed to them even stronger than the first. It was deeper, more disturbing, and very moving, with an even more surprising ending. Andy showed Dash a rough draft after three weeks, and he was bowled over by it.

"You two have an amazing way of combining your talents. You're an incredible team," Dash said to Andy after he read it. "Are you going to keep working with her after this one? You have a winning combo here," he said, in awe of the work he had just read.

"She's a gift from heaven," Andy said solemnly.

"You both are. You complement each other. Your writing each makes the other one's stronger. Don't mess with it, when something's working like this."

"I'm not." Violet and Andy argued about a detail sometimes, and the compromises they came to made the work even better.

And within a week of their return from LA, they were informed that they were nominated for an Academy Award. They were wildly excited about it, and kept working on their new film at a steady pace.

By the end of February, they had a finished script they were both happy with and Dash loved it. They were bowled over too by their Academy Award nomination for the first one. Violet thought they should go back for the ceremony, but Andy didn't, for a different reason this time.

"We won't win it, Vi. Not this time. The competition is too stiff, and some of them are really good, better than we are. I don't want to interrupt the work here just to show off on the red carpet. We don't need to." She didn't fight him as hard on it this time. She didn't want to interrupt the flow of their work either, and Dash was putting together lists of actors, which was important too. Henry Mason had agreed to direct again. And to go to LA with Godfrey to accept the award in case they won. They were going to stay at Andy's house. Andy wasn't afraid to go back to LA now. He had confronted his fears at the Golden Globes, and had overcome them. This time it was entirely about the work he and Violet had to do on their film, and not interrupting the flow. She thought he was right. She didn't want to leave either.

They loved working together, and reading what they wrote was like watching ballet. Andy had hit his stride with his writing, and Dash loved what they'd written, and so did the actors they'd submitted it to. Dash was working on putting together a fantastic cast in record time. He and Andy made the same agreement to coproduce, and this time Violet had written more of the actual script, and her writing was strong.

The actors who were available leapt at the chance

to make an indie movie with them. There were mostly Americans in the cast this time, and British ones who could do a credible American accent. It was an easy sell, with very possibly another award at the end of it.

As soon as they gave Dash the final script and they had a break, Andy started looking for a house for them. He found a charming mews house in a quiet fashionable street of mews houses in Knightsbridge, and Violet loved it when she saw it. He rented it for a year, and they moved two weeks later. It belonged to a famous British actor who was too old and infirm now to use it and had moved to the country. But he didn't want to give it up. It suited Violet and Andy perfectly, and it didn't occur to either of them that they could live separately. They needed to be together for their writing, and in countless other ways. It seemed natural to be together. Andy didn't know if he wanted to stay in England or go back to LA. All he knew for sure was that he loved Violet, and they loved their new home.

Dash was intrigued when he saw the house. "Are you planning to stay here?" he asked Andy when they were alone one afternoon in his office.

"I don't know. I haven't figured it out yet." It had been a year since he'd been fired, and his whole world had changed, his job and his life. He wasn't sure which life suited him better. There obviously wasn't going to be another studio head job for him, maybe not even in the distant future, and he loved the writing he and Violet did together. He had come a long way in a year. His pride would have liked another studio head job, but in his heart, he was happy where he was.

"Just let me know if you want me to stay at your place in LA for a year, you know, to keep things running smoothly, make sure the staff are doing their jobs. I'd do it as a favor, of course," Dash said, and Andy laughed and gave him a classic Hollywood answer.

"I'll get back to you on that," Andy said, and went home to his cozy carriage house, where Violet was waiting to do some more polishing on the script while they looked for the cast. A year after losing what he thought was the best job in the world, his life was very sweet. He didn't know if it was what he wanted to do forever, but for now it was perfect.

Chapter 16

Andy was right about the Academy Awards. They didn't win. It was a disappointment, but not a crushing one. He had never expected them to win this time, but even the nomination was a feather in their caps, and a victory of sorts. They were deep into auditions by then, and had half of the cast chosen, all of whom were wildly excited about the project. Dash and Andy had signed a new coproduction contract on the same terms. And Violet had written about a third of the screenplay this time. She was learning a lot from Andy, at a rapid rate. She couldn't have written it alone, but her contribution was important and valuable. Andy's screenwriting talent shone like diamonds in the script.

They both sat in on the auditions every day, and had a strong voice in the selections, and definite opinions. Violet knew the material like her own hand, since the concept had been hers to begin with. The characters had become more and more real to her as she and Andy wrote the script, and sometimes the obvious choice of actors felt wrong to her in her gut, which Andy and Dash respected. She had an unfailing sense of who would best bring the picture to life.

Dash wanted the cast selected and locked in by the first of April, with contracts signed rapidly. He was planning to start shooting the picture on the first of August to give them a month more than they had last time for shooting and postproduction. They were going to do preproduction in July. They were aiming for a Christmas release again, maybe slightly earlier than last time if they could pull it off. Despite his sometimes frighteningly casual air, and alarming style of dress, according to Andy, Dash ran a tight ship, and had respected all his target dates last time, and Andy was sure he would again. He used cajoling, threats, bribery, anything he had to do, to keep the film rolling on schedule. He and Andy were financing the production again, so they had no problems with investors. They had their system down pat this time and knew what pitfalls to avoid after the last one, which had run smoothly too. Their productions ran like a well-oiled machine. Everything was on schedule so far for their second film.

Andy had planned to take a week off after the

Academy Awards. Wendy's kids had a school vacation and he had convinced her to bring them to London for five days. He hadn't seen her since Thanksgiving. Peter had to work, but she and the children were excited about coming, while he and Violet were trying to figure out what to do with an eight- and six-year-old for five days, beyond the changing of the guard at Buckingham Palace, which Andy still loved and found fascinating. So far, they had figured out the Tower of London, Madame Tussaud's wax museum, and a children's museum Violet had read about. She knew more about that age group than he did, which was a delicate subject with her, and she never mentioned it. She was looking forward to the visit too, although it would be bittersweet for her, Andy knew, whether she said so or not, because of Liam. Jamie was almost the same age as Liam had been.

Violet and Wendy hadn't met yet, and a year after Violet had appeared in her father's life, Wendy had decided she'd better meet her, particularly since she was playing such a vital role in his work life now. She and Peter had discussed it, and to calm her concerns about an unknown woman in her father's life that she'd never even seen, Peter reminded her how vehemently her father was opposed to marriage, for himself. He thought it was fine for others, but he had no intention of repeating his earlier mistakes, nor of slowing down. Peter thought it highly unlikely that Andy, fifty-eight now, had gone soft on his earlier ban on marriage, and was sure he had warned Violet of it. He had warned all the other women in his life previously. But Wendy also reminded him that Violet was younger than his usual profile of women in their forties, or around fifty. He'd never been drawn to young girls, or much younger women, before Violet.

"She's thirty-nine," Wendy reminded him. "That's a lot younger than the others. What if she wants kids?"

"If she did, he wouldn't be dating her. He sees ours two or three times a year, he hardly ever saw you as a child. And she sounds like a workaholic like him. I guarantee you, babies are not in your dad's future, nor a bride. He had a hell of a shock last year, which reminded him of the fragility of big jobs in his industry, and I think he came out of it wanting to have a good time and enjoy his work. Getting fired like that, for a guy like him, strips you down to the bare bones, and makes you figure out what's important to you. In a way. It puts you face-to-face with your own mortality, professionally, and how replaceable you are, which is never a good feeling." As she always did, Wendy felt better after she talked to Peter. They had a good marriage. She had her parents' example of what not to do, although her mother's second marriage seemed to be a happy one, and her current husband was more of a family man than Andy had been.

When they arrived, Wendy was pleasantly surprised that Violet was nothing like what she had expected. Because of Violet's age, Wendy had assumed she was sexier, and probably bolder and brasher. And Wendy always worried about women's material ambitions around her father. He was generous, his wealth was obvious, and women in the film industry saw him as an opportunity for instant stardom and rapid advancement. Instead, she found Violet very quiet at first, somewhat shy. She looked young, but she dressed conservatively, more like her father. She was very sweet to the kids, had a warm, friendly way with them, and seemed to have a real gift with little boys. Jamie loved her, and Lizzie thought she was pretty. She was beautiful, Wendy recognized, but in a totally natural way. There was nothing ambitious or extravagant about her. She was passionate about her work, but she appeared to want to make it on her own merits, and not trade on Andy's.

The two women liked each other almost immediately, were casual and at ease with each other, and in a moment alone, Violet confided to her how proud her father was of her, and how much he loved her, even if he got easily distracted at times and didn't always seem as though he was paying attention. She said he spoke of her and the children constantly, and like a flower in the rain, or a woman who had been neglected by a too-busy

father as a child, Wendy blossomed when she heard
it. Her father's inattention had caused her to choose
a husband more carefully, and she had found a man
whose first priority was his family, according to the
values of his own family and how he'd grown up.

Wendy found Violet very shy at first, but she
warmed up and opened up day by day. In a bold
moment, when she and Violet took the children
to the zoo while Andy had a finance meeting with
Dash and their insurers, Wendy asked her if she
wanted children. Violet seemed to freeze when she
asked her, as though even the question was painful.

"I don't think so. That wouldn't work for me,"
she said without further explanation. In fact, the
idea of losing another child she loved was so frightening and unbearable that she couldn't even remotely imagine taking that risk again. Liam had
been her one and only great love. He was not
replaceable, and she didn't want to try. She had
changed the subject immediately, but Wendy was
reassured by her answer.

Wendy brought it up casually to her father, one
night when they went to pick up dinner together
and Violet was watching the kids. Wendy was telling him how much she liked her, that she was a real
person, and so sweet to the children. "And at least
she doesn't want any of her own. That must be a
relief to you, Dad, with a woman her age." He had
recently turned fifty-eight, and with a woman nineteen years younger, children were presumably an

issue, or could prove to be, especially since Violet had none. Wendy had always disliked the idea that he might have other children one day. He hadn't been present for her, and it upset her to think of his being more attentive to a second generation of children with a new wife. Even the mention of it made her jealous.

"How do you know that she doesn't want children?" Andy asked her as they stood in line, waiting to buy pizza for the kids. They had wanted to stay home for dinner, and play at Grampa's house. Wendy and the children were staying at Claridge's, because the carriage house was too small for three guests. Andy had never dared broach the delicate subject of future children with Violet, because of Liam.

"I asked her," Wendy said blithely, "you know, girl talk. She's almost my age, she loves you, and it's a reasonable question." Violet was six years older than Wendy, but seemed infinitely wiser and more mature to Andy, and had had a much harder life.

"She had a son," he said quietly. "He died in an accident four years ago, when he was a few months younger than Jamie. He died because of his father's dangerously risky behavior. He was driving at a high speed on ice, and hadn't put on the boy's seat belt." Andy sounded somber when he said it, and Wendy looked horrified.

"Oh my God." She looked pale at the image he painted. "The poor woman. Oh God, Dad, the poor thing. How did she survive it? That would kill me."

"I think it almost killed her. She's a strong woman, and there's a lot more to her than one sees at first. She got me through the last year. She got me writing again. I hired her as an assistant, and I found a manuscript she was working on. We turned it into a screenplay together. I've never talked to her about wanting more kids. I don't get the impression she wants more. I think it was too painful when she lost her son." It suddenly explained to Wendy how naturally at ease she was with Jamie. She knew little boys that age. Wendy looked serious when she and her father left the pizza parlor with three boxes of pizza, with her children's favorite toppings and combinations.

"I'm really sorry, Dad, that I brought up the subject. I like her. A lot. I can see why you do too. She's not some gold digger out to play you, like Alana and all the movie stars before her. To them, dating is a business." He laughed and it lightened the moment. He felt sad for Violet that Wendy had brought up the question of children to her.

"You should see who Alana's dating now. The oldest studio head in the business. He's a terrible curmudgeon. He's been married four times to girls in their twenties, and Alana won't be the next one." He laughed and truly didn't care. The wounds of the last year had healed nicely. He was comfortable in his own skin as never before, and Wendy could see it. And if it was thanks to Violet, she was grateful.

In their five days in London, they took the children to the zoo, a carnival, a boat ride on the Thames, an interactive children's museum Violet had found, a doll museum for Lizzie, a military museum for Jamie, and a teddy bear factory where they made their own bears they could take home. And Andy had participated in most of it and had made the time to do so, more than ever before. What Wendy noticed about him that was different was that Violet had humanized him. He was just as passionate about his work, but it was hands-on, it challenged him, he was collaborative with Violet. He didn't seem to be interested in showing off anymore. He had always been a real person under the big job, but now he was more down-to-earth. And he seemed much happier in his life than he had been before.

He had always been running, but to what? Now he had real goals, with the movies he was making, and he was achieving them, which gave him more satisfaction. He said himself that he wasn't sure what he would do in the future, but for now, he felt like he was exactly where he should be. He confirmed that he was keeping his house in LA, in case he went back, and he had urged Wendy to use it if she wanted to. Her family had stayed there when she and Peter took the children to Disneyland over a long weekend, and had commuted to Anaheim

from his house, which was better than any hotel
with the gigantic pool. Andy was more than willing
to share his blessings with his only child, and her
children. The visit to London had been fun for all
of them.

Andy drove Wendy and the children to the airport himself when they left, which was a first.
Violet came with him, and they went from the airport to work for more auditions.

Dash had selected two more members of the
cast in the last five days. Violet and Andy hadn't
missed much.

Wendy and her children would remember the
visit forever. They could all coast on that for a
long time, and Andy had urged Wendy again to
bring them out in the summer, in July, before they
started shooting, if the children didn't go to camp
again. Both of the kids were clutching the new
bears they'd made when they left. Jamie had named
his Andy, and Lizzie had named hers Violet, and
tied a lavender bow around her neck, when Wendy
told her what "violet" meant. The visit had been
a smash hit. Wendy sent her father an email that
said so clearly and thanked them for the wonderful time they'd had with both him and Violet. He
had tears in his eyes when he read it and showed
it to Violet. She was deeply touched too. She and
Wendy had become friends in a real way.

Andy and Violet settled down in earnest in the
days after Wendy and the children left. In the next

week, they picked the rest of the cast. Contracts were drawn up, negotiated, and adjusted. They had everything sewn up ahead of schedule in late March, and they were sticking to the projected shooting schedule, with preproduction in July, and they would start filming on the first of August. It was all nice and tidy and falling into place.

Andy and Violet were talking about some of the preproduction details when they got home that night. It was six o'clock in London and ten A.M. in LA, when Andy's lawyer, Barry Weiss, called him. He sounded serious, as he usually did. He wasn't a jolly kind of guy, but he was a good lawyer, especially with complicated contracts.

"Did you see the newspaper today?" he asked Andy.

"No, did the stock market crash? Should I be panicked?" Andy always tried to lighten Barry's dark moods, usually without success. "Is something wrong?" Andy asked more seriously.

"There was a plane crash over the weekend, a private jet. Harvey Seligman was on it. Everyone on the plane died, including Seligman and his wife. You obviously know he was the head of Planet Z," the second biggest studio in the business after Global, and neck-and-neck recently, with the new head of Global losing ground, predictably. "I just got a call from the chairman of their parent company. To cut to the chase, they want you, Andy. Badly. They'll pay almost any price. They need you desperately.

They have a lot of big deals on the table, and no CEO. They need you to start immediately."

"The king is dead, long live the king," Andy said softly, taking it all in.

"If you want it, you're back in, on top, where you belong. It's a fantastic studio. They'll give you carte blanche. It's what you've been waiting for, and the opportunity won't come again. This is a fluke. No one leaves those head of studio jobs unless they get fired or die. And you're not going to want to be fooling around with little indie films for the rest of your career. You have nothing else to do right now. But this is what you do, Andy, and the job you want." Barry told Andy the dollar amount Planet Z had quoted as a starting point for negotiations, and it was breathtaking, even more than he'd made before, which was hard to imagine. "You're the only man they want for the job. Your noncompete expired five days ago, so the timing is perfect. They want you to come to LA as fast as you can get here to talk to them. They'll send a plane for you." It was one hell of a powerful message Barry had delivered, and Andy was silent for a minute.

"It was considerate of Harvey to get in a plane crash five days after my noncompete expires," he said ironically. There was something so sad and so sordid about it. A man and his wife that Andy knew had died. They weren't close friends, they were competitors, but Andy knew and respected Harvey. He had children and grandchildren who loved him, presumably. The crew and several other passengers had died too, and they were talking about Andy's severance contract, his noncompete, and how much Planet Z were willing to pay him. It was business above all else. But if he wanted to be a studio head again, Barry was right, this was his chance. It didn't get better than this. And a man "only" had to die to make it happen.

"How fast can you get here?" Barry asked him.

"I don't know," Andy said vaguely. He felt totally turned around and stunned by the news, sad for Harvey and his wife and the others. A door had opened that Andy had wanted so desperately, and he wasn't sure how he felt about it now. He felt shocked and numb. If he took it, playtime was over and he'd be king again, at an even better job than he had before, for more money. And Planet Z was an impeccably run company, much better than Global these days. Global had an inexperienced CEO, and a year later it had started to show. There was no victory in it for Andy. He didn't want revenge or retribution, he just hated to see a company he had once loved and put so much effort into start to slip.

"I have to call you back," he told Barry. It was early on the West Coast, so he had time. He needed to catch his breath. He hung up and looked at Violet.

"Is something wrong?" she asked him. He didn't look elated, and she saw the shock on his face. He told her what had happened, and she was suddenly quiet. There was no doubt in her mind what he had to do. It wasn't even a question for her. "You have to take it, Andy. This is what you've been waiting for. It won't happen again." He knew it too. How many plane crashes would there be to wipe out the rival studio heads and free up their seats for him?

"Christ, Vi, I feel like we're going through the wreckage, and going through Harvey's pockets and stealing his job. Talk about being vultures or predators. The poor man isn't cold yet, and they want to hire me. They don't waste any time." But it was yet another multibillion-dollar corporation and they needed a CEO immediately.

"When do they want you to go?"

"Now," he said dismally.

"Was he young?" Violet asked.

"Not really, but not ancient. Seventy-two, seventy-three, that's not old these days in business. He was a strong, vital force, and he wasn't going anywhere. He ran the place like a machine, and he was tough. This is just so fast. I wasn't expecting it. I gave up the idea of another job like mine months ago. And now they're offering me another even better one, and I'm supposed to run out of here, put on a suit, and step into the job. We're making a movie, I can't just walk out on that, and on you, and I don't want to. I want to do this with you. You turned down an opportunity for a series to do it, and now I just run out the door and go back to LA? It's like **Groundhog Day.** It'll be like I never left, and I don't even know if I want that kind of job anymore." That was the crux of it. Andy had changed, just enough that he didn't quite fit in the old mold anymore. But the film industry hadn't changed, it was the same, and as ruthless as ever. He didn't want to be ruthless anymore. But what else would he do? Maybe Barry was right and he'd get bored with writing screenplays for indie movies, but he liked doing it with Violet.

"And what about you? You stay here to shoot the film and I go back?" he asked her.

"We'll figure it out. We'll make it work if we have to," she said kindly. She wanted his happiness first.

"Maybe that kind of job is over for me. I did it. I sacrificed a marriage and a daughter to do it, and everything else. I don't know if I want to do it again. And if I do, it says that I learned nothing in the last year. I had fun making an indie movie, won an award, and now I'd be going back for more of the same." He was the perfect example of "beware of what you wish for," and Violet wanted to be careful not to influence him and hold him back. He had to do what was right for him. She loved him enough to want the best for him.

He went out for a walk, and came back an hour later. He looked unhappy and tormented instead of thrilled. If he wanted to, he could be a studio head again by the next day, but he didn't know what he wanted. He called Dash and told him when he got back from his walk. Violet was lying low, in her little study, drinking a cup of tea. Dash was as shocked as Andy had been.

"Boy, those guys don't fool around, do they?"

"No, they don't. They didn't fool around with me a year ago either."

"I guess you don't have any choice," Dash said sadly. "You'll always regret it if you don't go back. You won't get another chance like this, Andy. It's a once-in-a-lifetime opportunity. You'll never make that kind of money making indies, or have that kind of power. And power is your gig. That's why it hurt you so much when you lost it. Making indies you're down here with the real people like me. We don't wear suits, shave, or brush our hair. You've been living on the top of Olympus for twenty years with the gods and kingmakers. That's tough to give up. You've been a good sport about it. But they're giving you a chance to return from the dead. It won't come again. I think you'll be miserable a year, two years, ten from now, if you turn it down. You should probably go back. When do they want you?"

"Yesterday. It would be immediate. I can negotiate a few weeks, but they need someone to run the place. It's a vast entity, as big as Global now. Harvey did a good job."

"Poor bastard. All you fancy guys, you're safer flying commercial." Andy smiled at the comment. "What does Vi say?"

"That I should do what's best for me."

"She loves you," Dash said. "I don't love you like she does, but I want what's right for you too. I can manage the production of the picture without you. You've already written the script. Vi can handle any changes and corrections, and she can discuss them with you if she needs to. You can go to LA to talk to them if you want to. You won't kill the picture, so don't let that stop you. I hate like hell to lose you and to see you go back to that rat race of people trying to kill you. I don't want that life myself, but you're a power guy. I've come to understand that about you. You're a born CEO. Do whatever you need to do. Life is too short to waste it on a job you hate, and too long to miss out on a job you'd probably love. I'll miss you like crazy if you leave, but you have my blessing either way." Andy was touched by what he said.

"They want me to come and talk to them," Andy said unhappily.

"You may have to do that, unless you're ready to turn them down flat, which could be insane for the kind of money they'd pay you. You need to smell the air and get a feel for the company, and see what you think," Dash said sensibly. He was being very fair. He had a lot to lose if Andy left and took the job.

"I think this is more about me than about them, and what I want now. It's been a lot of changes in a year, especially at my age. I'm fifty-eight. What do

I really want to do with the next two or twenty-five or even thirty years if I'm blessed?"

"I'm not sure that's relevant. Harvey could have been forty and he'd be just as dead. You can't predict these things. I think it's more about what you want now. Who are you? What do **you** want?"

"If you figure that out, call me," Andy said glumly. "I think I'll fly out to see them tomorrow and get it over with. With the time difference in that direction, I can meet with them tomorrow and figure it out fast."

Dash hesitated for a minute. "Andy, one piece of advice. Do what **you** want. Don't turn this down if you really want it. You'll regret it forever and it won't come again. I know you. You're a born studio head. You're not a down-on-the-ground guy like me."

"Why? Because I brush my hair and wear a shirt?"

"You just are. You're a king, Andy. You're not a foot soldier. You belong up there with the gods of the industry. Just put in a good word for me when you get there. Have a safe trip. May the Force be with you," he said, quoting **Star Wars.** He was such a good guy and Andy knew he'd miss working with him if he went back to running a studio. But Planet Z was a good one and he respected it. He would be proud to run it. It wasn't just a job. It was a strong career move.

He called Barry back after he talked to Dash. "Tell them I can fly in tomorrow. They can probably have the plane here in the morning if they send it now. I'll be ready to go when the plane gets here, so I could see them in the early afternoon in LA. I want to get this over with quickly." He wanted to make a decision fast, and either go to the job in LA or continue his life here.

"You don't sound happy about it." Barry was surprised.

"I don't know what I am. That's the problem."

"I'll let you know when the plane will be there. Do you want me to come to the meeting with you?" he volunteered.

"Maybe. I'll let you know."

He texted Andy a few minutes later. The plane would be ready for a ten A.M. departure in the area for private planes at Heathrow. Andy was familiar with it.

He lay in bed wide-awake that night. That morning his life had been so simple. He was making a movie and working with the woman he loved. Now everything was complicated. He had choices. Hard choices. He could go back in time to a job and a world he understood, where he had status and power and was paid a fortune. A job where he would have little time for a personal life. A world where they could stop everything and throw him out from one second to the next. They had before and they would again if it served their interests, but it wouldn't surprise him as much the next time if they did. In the end, it was more about the power than the money. The ephemeral ingredient that made those jobs so addictive. He had loved the power when he had it. He couldn't deny it. And he still missed it.

Now he had no power, but he had a life he loved, doing work he enjoyed, that made him feel good about himself, with a good woman at his side. Violet wouldn't leave him if he opted for the power job now, she would stick by him, but they'd be apart a lot. It boiled down to whether he wanted to live among the mortals, like a real person, or go back up the mountain and live among the gods, knowing that they could throw him off a cliff anytime. It should have been an easy decision. But it wasn't. It was the hardest decision of his life, a choice about who he wanted to be when he grew up. But he was grown up, and the game was almost over for him. What game did he want to play? And how did he want the story to end? Those were the key questions now.

Andy lay holding Violet as she slept, and he got up at six o'clock and showered and dressed. He was dressed for the trip when she woke up and came out to the kitchen, naked under a pink satin robe.

"If you come in here dressed like that, I won't leave," he said, and she smiled and sat down at the table across from him and held his hand.

"Did you sleep?" she asked him, worried about him. She knew how challenging this was for him, and how hard the decision. He looked tormented.

"Not much," he said. "When Global fired me, I lost all respect for myself. Now I'll lose the self-respect I've found if I go back. I don't know if I want to be that person anymore. I like myself better now."

"I love you either way," Violet said firmly. "Do what **you want.** That's all you need to figure out. Everyone will adjust, and so will I." Andy needed that reassurance from her and was grateful to have it. She always gave him what he needed and said the right things.

He left a few minutes later. A car came to take him to the plane. Planet Z had sent the car, a Rolls with a driver. They made it all so easy and so tempting, and eventually you bought into it and believed it was real. But he knew now it wasn't, and it didn't last. One day it all disappeared, and it all turned to dust in your hands, and you turned to dust with it. He felt whole again. It had taken a year and he hated to give that up. But having power again was a tremendous lure and hard to resist.

He held Violet for a last time at the door. "I wish you were coming with me," he said, feeling like a little boy and not a man.

"You can do this, Andy. You'll make the right decision. I have total faith in you." As he heard the words, they were the same words his father would have said to him and often had.

"I love you. I'll be back tomorrow." Violet didn't know if he would or not, and neither did he, as he hurried out the door and walked to the car. He didn't turn back to look at her or she would have seen the tears in his eyes. He felt as though he was being asked to give up everything he'd built in the last year. What he had built was a part of himself he had never known before. Who he was without the power and the status, who he really was as a man. And if he went back that was what he had to give up. And part of him still wanted the power so badly. He was ashamed of how much he still wanted it. He could taste it. But the man he had become didn't want it and was telling him to run. He didn't know whether to run forward or back. He knew both worlds now, the old and the new, and there was a life and death battle going on within him. He couldn't be both men. He had to choose one. And whichever he chose, he'd have to give up the other part of himself forever. It was an agonizing decision.

Chapter 17

When Violet got to Dash's studio that morning, she looked serious, and he showed up in her office a few minutes later.

"Did he go?" he asked her, and she nodded.

"He's on the plane now." She looked sad but resigned.

"What do you think he'll do?" Dash asked her.

"I don't know. I think he should take the job and go back. He'll always regret it if he doesn't. He's meant to be in that world. It cost him so much when they took it all away. It was like ripping his heart out."

Dash nodded. He didn't disagree. "They'll do it to him again if they want to. You're never safe in that world."

"I don't want him to regret it if he doesn't go back. He thrives on the power. He was lost without it. It's taken him a year to find himself. He might not recover next time. But not taking back the power, he might lose his life force," she said wisely. She knew him well.

"As much as I hate that world, I think he should go back too," Dash said, although he knew that power could be a very empty thing. He went back to his own office then, and he and Violet tried to concentrate on their work all day, with little success. Violet knew she wouldn't hear from Andy that night. He would be landing in London at eight P.M. London time, which would only be noon in LA. The meetings which would ultimately decide his future would begin at two P.M. in LA, ten in London, and would end hours later. His fate wouldn't be decided until the next day in London. It was going to be a very long twenty-four hours for her. She had no idea which man would be coming home to her, if he even came home. He might stay and start the job right away. But would he be the man she knew and loved now, or the one he had been before that she had never met?

Planet Z's Boeing Triple 777 landed at LAX at twelve-fifteen P.M. The plane they had lost over the weekend was brought down by a bird strike. It seemed so crazy that a flock of birds could bring down a plane that size and kill half a dozen people. Andy thought about Harvey, the late studio head, on the trip, and wondered what he would advise him, knowing the company and the job, and the shape the studio was in. As far as Andy knew it ran smoothly, but there were always hidden elements he couldn't see, and problems they didn't tell you if they wanted you for the job. He was awake for the entire flight, thinking.

He was through with Customs and Immigration by one o'clock local time.

A chauffeured limousine met him at LAX and drove him to Planet Z. He'd been able to shower and change on the flight. He was wearing a dark suit, a white shirt, and a tie, as he always did. On sight of the familiar landscape of LA, and all the swimming pools they'd flown over, he felt like he was home again. He was going to sleep in his own bed in Bel-Air that night. He wasn't going back to London until the next day.

There was an entire team of people waiting for him in the lobby of Planet Z when he walked in. The décor was as spectacular as he had expected it to be, with planets and satellites hanging from the thirty-foot ceiling in an entirely black granite lobby with an enormous twenty-foot bronze Z in the center of it. The team escorted him upstairs to the executive floor, where top management was waiting for him, and his own office would be. They had cleared it that morning of all of Harvey's things, which had already been delivered to his home. They had moved quickly so there was no trace of tragedy when Andy arrived. The meeting was about the future of Planet Z, not the past. And a full buffet had been set out on a long sideboard in the conference room.

The entire legal team was there. They already had contracts drawn up, which could be modified instantly. Barry Weiss had already received a draft of the contract digitally and was waiting in his office. The chairman and CEO of the parent company were there at the Planet Z offices to clinch the deal, and so were the most important department heads that Andy would be directing and would want to meet. They were fully prepared to woo him, and the entrance package they were offering him was dazzling, with a list of perks ten pages long. It was a deal that not a single person in the film industry could resist. They were incredibly smooth.

When Andy stepped off the elevator, the escort team disappeared. The chairman of the parent company, and the CEO, a woman, stepped forward to greet him, and asked how the flight was. They pointed out the meal set up for him, but he said he had eaten on the plane. Andy was suddenly reminded of a meeting his father had described to him once when he was screenwriting in the beginning, and the studio wanted to talk him into something he didn't want to do. His father had said, "Son, just remember, all horseshit smells the same, no matter how fine-looking the horse." And it was so true. Andy had to struggle to keep a straight face, but it had relaxed him to think of his father. And Planet Z had some fine-looking horses.

The chairman and CEO of the parent company did a very impressive presentation, telling him all about Planet Z, their current status, and plans for the future. The department heads at the meeting were equally impressive, and each of them spoke for a few minutes and Andy could see they would be interesting to work with. They were all extremely bright people. No mention was made of Harvey Seligman, their late CEO, although he'd been in the job for fourteen years and they must have had some attachment to him. The CFO handed him a sealed envelope with their final financial offer, which encompassed everything, and their chief counsel handed him another copy of the contract to look over. They had done absolutely everything in their power to make the job as attractive as possible to him.

On the list of perks in his contract, in an itemized memorandum, he saw that he would have a Triple 777 Boeing for his personal use, available at all times.

The chairman cleared his throat and spoke when he saw that Andy was on that page, since they were sitting next to each other.

"We're down a plane at the moment," he explained. "But it will be replaced by the end of the week," obviously the one that had gone down with Harvey only days before. Even that was being speedily remedied and replaced with no mention of their late CEO.

"Would you like to see your office?" the female CEO of the owning company offered in a motherly tone, and they trooped down a locked hall with a security guard at its entrance to show it to him, no doubt the same security guard who would escort him to the street if he were ever fired. He couldn't get that memory out of his head from a year before, being walked out of the building with a guard on each side of him.

They went back to the conference room, and the chief counsel offered him a pen, if he was ready to sign. Andy held it in his hand for a moment and looked around the table at all of them. He was tired from the trip, and he had been there for three hours during their presentation.

"I'm sure you all know who my father was, John Westfield. He was from Montana, a genuine cowboy. And he always told me never to sign a deal without sleeping on it. It's good advice, and I've stuck to it all my life. The deal you're offering me is an absolutely magnificent package. There is nothing I'd want to change, although I'd like to discuss it with my attorney. You've been generous in the extreme, and I'm honored to be here, and by what you're offering me. But I'd like to sleep on it before I sign. I'd like to honor my father and all of you by signing when I'm wide-awake and rested and have given it very serious thought. To be honest, I thought my days as a studio head were gone forever. These jobs come up once in a blue moon, if then. And I'm very sorry about what happened to Harvey Seligman and his wife, and that his tragedy would be my opportunity, but above all I'm grateful to you for offering me a way back, and I hope to do you proud if I accept it. You'll have my answer at nine o'clock tomorrow morning." They told him they already had, to speed up the process. With that Andy stood up and shook hands all around the table. There were eleven people in the room, and the parent company chairman and CEO walked him to the elevator and the escort team materialized magically again to take him downstairs. He could see the anxious looks on their faces when he left, but he needed the night and time alone to give him counsel.

There was not a single thing wrong with the deal. Maybe there was something wrong with him, but he didn't want to leap into their arms without being absolutely sure that he wanted the job and everything that went with it. He crossed the impressive black granite lobby and looked up at the twenty-foot bronze Z and wondered if this would be his new home for the rest of his career, and how long it would last. Would it go the distance or be short-term? It was the first time he had ever asked himself that question.

The Planet Z Rolls took him to his house in

Bel-Air, where Timothy was waiting for him. It was two A.M. in London by then, much too late to call Violet or anyone else.

He had Timothy make him a martini. All he wanted was a simple sandwich, a shower, and bed. He didn't even have time to think about the deal or how he felt about it. He was too tired to think. He was in bed less than an hour later, and had asked Timothy to wake him at seven. It gave him two hours to make the decision once he woke up. He thought he'd be ready by then. He was too tired now to think clearly. And there was no question, the deal they were offering him was dazzling.

Jet-lagged, he woke up at six, and checked his emails. Barry, his lawyer, had approved the contract and said it was the best deal of its kind he'd ever seen. There was a separate package built in, with a two-year severance and two-year noncompete, which Barry thought was acceptable, given how high Andy's annual salary would be, considerably higher than it was at Global.

There was not a single thing wrong with the deal.

Andy walked out to the pool and swam laps for a while to clear his head. There was no one around at that hour, so he swam naked, wrapped himself in a towel when he came out, and sat in a lounge chair, thinking. It was the same chair where he had fallen asleep drunk every night for two weeks after he was

fired and his world disintegrated around him, and
his ego, which had taken the hardest hit. Now his
head was clear, and he had a woman he loved and
who loved him in his life. It was a lot. More than
enough. And he had found himself, which was important too. It had taken him a year of sorrow and
despair and fear and shame, but he wasn't ashamed
of the past anymore, or afraid of the future.

He walked past the poster of his father on the
way to his room after he swam and saluted him.
"Hi, Dad."

He shaved, showered, dressed, and wrote the
most important email of his life. He thanked
Planet Z for their magnificent offer and said that
he didn't feel returning to a job he'd been away
from for a year now, and which had been painful
to lose, fit into his current career plans. And with
gratitude and appreciation for their consideration,
he declined. He said that at this time, he didn't feel
he was the right man for the job. He sat and looked
at it for a long quiet moment, read it several times,
and then pressed Send. He was sure now. It was the
right decision for him. The price of all that power
was too high. He didn't want it or need it as much
as he'd thought anymore. He wanted to make movies and write screenplays, not run the world from
a mountaintop wielding unlimited power. He
wanted to be a man, not one of the gods.

Andy forwarded a copy of the email to Barry and
asked him to keep it confidential. He called the

phone number the pilot had given him to confirm his departure time. They were due to take off at ten A.M. They would land in London at eight P.M. LA time, which was five A.M. local London time the next day. He shook hands with Timothy when he left.

"I hope to see you soon, sir."

"You will at some point," Andy said. He took his own car to the airport, with a driver Timothy had hired, and they reached the Planet Z plane on time. The chairman called him before the flight took off and tried to convince him to reconsider.

"A year ago, I'd have grabbed it with both hands in a minute. I prayed for a job like this one. But things change in a year. I changed. It's not the right place or the right job for me anymore. I wish it was," and he honestly did for a moment. He wished he were still that man, but he wasn't. The power wasn't enough to compensate him for all he had to give up, mostly himself. He thanked the chairman again for the opportunity, and the use of the plane. They took off a few minutes later. This time, he slept for most of the flight. He had done all his thinking, and he was at peace. As crazy as it sounded, he knew he had made the right decision. The money had been fabulous, but he would have paid with his soul and his life in exchange. It just wasn't worth it to him anymore.

*   *   *

The plane landed in London half an hour early. Andy thanked the pilot, copilot, and flight attendants for the easy flight, and he took a cab from the airport to the mews house in Knightsbridge. He was a mere mortal now, not a god. The clock had struck midnight, and the coachmen had turned into white mice. He had an Indian driver who told him all about his family in Mumbai, and he arrived at the house at five-thirty, and let himself quietly into the house. He hadn't spoken to Violet since he left because of the time difference, and there was too much to say. He knew she'd still be asleep. He tiptoed up the stairs to their bedroom, undressed, and got into bed next to her, and felt the silk of her skin next to his.

She stirred sleepily and half-opened one eye. "You're back!" she said softly, and smiled at him as he took her in his arms.

"I turned it down," he whispered to her and kissed her. Her eyes opened wide then.

"You did? Are you sure that's what you want?"

"Completely," he said with absolutely certainty. "We'll talk about it later," he said, and made love to her, happy that he was just a man, not a god.

Chapter 18

Violet and Andy's second film started shooting right on schedule on August first in Dash's studio outside London. The early scenes were often the hardest, but they were off to a good start, as Andy and Violet sat side by side in the directors' chairs with copies of the script in their hands, to make sure that the actors didn't improvise, change something, or stray from the sense of the scenes on the page. It was a sunny day, but it was nighttime on the set, as Andy glanced at Violet and she smiled, and they held hands for a minute.

It had been seventeen months since he'd been fired by Global Studios, and five since he had turned down Planet Z's exorbitant offer to reinstate him as one of Hollywood's most powerful men. Instead they were writing screenplays together and making movies. The only power he had was over his pen, to do a good job. And the only person who could fire him was Violet, as her writing partner. He was happy. Happier than he'd ever been, and so was she. They were creating something, and building something that would last, movies that would mean something to people and that they would remember, like his father's films, which were classics and people still loved them.

The power Andy had wielded for so many years had turned out to be ephemeral. It meant nothing. It was smoke and mirrors. It had been an illusion. His life was real now, and his work. He could imagine making movies with Violet long into the future, indies, or with a studio one day. Or maybe they'd do a TV series together if they went back to LA after the movie they were just starting, which was on schedule to be released at Christmas.

He had lost everything for a while, himself mostly, and had found himself again, altered, changed, metamorphosed, bigger, deeper. The life he had now was real, and so was Violet. They were battle-scarred and stronger for where they had been. And the crushing losses they'd experienced had taught them a great deal, and to be grateful for what they had.

The illusion of power had been a dream. He had woken up now. The world was bigger, better, and more beautiful than he had ever imagined. There was nothing more he wanted or needed than what he had right now. This second act of his career filled every day with joy. It was worth more than anything he'd ever had before. He wouldn't have given it up, or traded it, for anything in the world.

He leaned over and kissed Violet's cheek as she focused on the script they had created together. There would be more in the future. She looked up when he kissed her and smiled. In losing everything for a time, they had found each other, and all that mattered most in life.

About the Author

DANIELLE STEEL has been hailed as one of the world's bestselling authors, with a billion copies of her novels sold. Her many international bestsellers include **Happiness, Palazzo, The Wedding Planner, Worthy Opponents, Without a Trace, The Whittiers, The High Notes,** and other highly acclaimed novels. She is also the author of **His Bright Light,** the story of her son Nick Traina's life and death; **A Gift of Hope,** a memoir of her work with the homeless; **Expect a Miracle,** a book of her favorite quotations for inspiration and comfort; **Pure Joy,** about the dogs she and her family have loved; and the children's books **Pretty Minnie in Paris** and **Pretty Minnie in Hollywood.**

daniellesteel.com
Facebook.com/DanielleSteelOfficial
Twitter: @daniellesteel
Instagram: @officialdaniellesteel

LIKE WHAT YOU'VE READ?

Try these titles by Danielle Steel,
also available in large print:

Palazzo
ISBN 978-0-593-58786-7

Happiness
ISBN 978-0-593-58787-4

The Wedding Planner
ISBN 978-0-593-58790-4

For more information on large print titles, visit
www.penguinrandomhouse.com/large-print-format-books